OBLIVION THRESHOLD

THE OBLIVION SAGA • BOOK ONE

J.R. MABRY
B.J. WEST

Apocryphile Press
1700 Shattuck Ave #81, Berkeley, CA 94709
www.apocryphilepress.com

Copyright © 2018 by J.R. Mabry & B.J. West
Printed in the United States of America
ISBN 978-1-947826-81-6 | paperback
ISNB 978-1-949643-41-1 | epub

GET THE BACK STORY...

Curious about this "Operation Catskill" everyone keeps
mentioning? Get read in on the classified mission!
Download the free prequel short story,
OPERATION CATSKILL today at
BookHip.com/FZBGP

The one principle of hell is "I am my own."
—George McDonald

PROLOGUE

[STRING 310]

The creature reared back, beholding Stan with its hundred eyes, the hairs around its mandibles quivering. It assumed a fighting stance, but just as Stan stabbed his thumb at it, it retreated into a seam of the navigation control panel.

"Lemme guess—spider lives to torment you another day," Tag teased him, her lips turning up in a mocking smile.

Stan fumed. He never seemed to be quick enough. There were a thousand spiders on this ship, and it seemed they all lived to torment him personally.

"Focus, people. Remember: first contact." Captain Santos' voice was kind but firm, but Stan needed no reminding. Neither did Tag. From the moment they'd detected the alien vessels headed their way, no one talked about anything else.

At first, they'd thought it was just an asteroid, big and fast. But projections showed it would shoot past the Manila Colony without causing any damage—until it changed course and began accelerating. That's when they knew it was a ship, and not a Colonial Defense ship, either. As the object got closer, they realized it was actually a plurality of objects—not a ship, but a *fleet* of ships moving in an almost impossibly tight formation.

At first, people had gone crazy—terrified that it was an attack. But as they got closer, analytics announced that there were no weapons aboard—at least none that they could detect, none that were even remotely like ours. People had relaxed. They became giddy, even. They had outfitted a small passenger liner, *The Avalon*, as a diplomatic vessel and rechristened her the *The Envoy*. And they were on their way to welcome the first sentient species humans had yet encountered. Tag had made party hats out of plastic hygiene sheathing, but one arched eyebrow from the captain had nixed that idea.

Stan checked the flight controls just to be sure he hadn't messed anything up in his arachnidicidal rage. No. They were sitting perfectly still, directly in the path of the oncoming fleet. Stan felt his muscles relax—a bit.

"I keep imagining what they'll be like," Tag whispered.

"Uh-huh. And what are they like?" Stan asked, not really paying attention.

"Oh, you know, all muscly and shit. Green maybe. *Big*. Big parts, too." He shook his head at her erotic fantasies, but in his peripheral vision he saw her do a weapons check.

"Captain!" Science Chief Andrada shouted curtly. "They are dropping out of superluminal."

"On screen, please."

The forward viewer switched to an external view, where several ships snapped into view.

"What the fuck?" Captain Santos rose from his command chair and took a couple steps, squinting at the screen. "Katz, zoom in on the oncoming fleet—maximum power."

The viewscreen refocused, and when it did, Stan gasped.

"Why are these ships…shimmering?"

It was true. Stan hadn't noticed it before they'd zoomed in, but it was obvious now. The surface of the ships reminded him of moonlight on a lake when the winds were high—the choppy surface rippling with light…just exactly as these were doing.

"What are we seeing, Andrada?"

"Checking, sir."

Stan saw the science officer close one eye as his hands flew over his panel, no doubt checking one bank of sensors on his neural while running all manner of remote analyses on his console. Time seemed to stand still as they waited. In the meantime, the rippling surface of the ships became larger, more defined, more turbulent.

"Andrada, I need some answers," the captain barked.

"Sorry, sir, I'm…the hull surfaces aren't like any metal or alloy we know of. But what we're seeing…isn't the surface."

"If it isn't the surface, what the fuck is it?"

Stan felt the hair on the back of his arms and neck rise up. He noticed he was holding his breath. He forced himself to exhale.

"Sir, I can't say with certainty. But I can tell you what it looks like."

"For Christ's sake, spit it out."

"From everything I see here, we aren't actually looking at the ships' *hulls*. We're seeing what looks like beings fixed to the hulls…or *clinging* to the hulls."

"Do you mean to tell me, Andrada, that these aliens travel on the outside of their ships rather than the inside?"

"It would appear so, sir. Yes."

Stan glanced at the captain. His eyebrows bunched in confusion. "How can that possibly—"

"Sir, I've got something else. It's too small to see visually just yet, but sensors show that a number of the...aliens, I guess...have launched themselves from the hull and are...god, they're headed right for us."

"Maybe this is how they say 'hello'?" Stan offered.

"Maybe this is how they say 'Die, bitch,'" the captain answered. "Target weapons."

"Targeting weapons, sir," Tag said. "I've got a lock on the lead alien, and the next five...God, sir—"

"Navigation, get us out of here. Anywhere *except* back to New Manila."

Stan shut his eyes and plotted a course through his neural. He implemented it internally and then opened his eyes again. He watched the star horizon on his panel swing as the ship came about. He tapped out minor course corrections manually as the granular information from stellar cartography began to feed into his brain. *Don't slam into an asteroid while we're making our escape*, he told himself.

"Scans show 759 aliens have now launched themselves toward us," Andrada's voice was pitched much higher than usual and Stan could hear the panic in it. "Oh...make that 15,657."

Someone whistled. Stan couldn't tell who.

"Fire at will, Lieutenant," Captain Santos ordered. "Wide sweep. Get as many of those bastards as you can. Engines to full now! GO! GO! GO!"

"Sir, how can any species survive in the vacuum of space?" Reyes asked.

"I'll be as fascinated as you are to hear how the xenobiologists explain that, Commander."

"Sir, we're accelerating as hard as we can, and rigging for

superluminal," Stan said. He could hear the distant whine of the engines climbing in pitch.

"They're gaining on us, Sir." Andrada said. "Our speed is 500K and climbing…nearly 600K now."

"And their speed?"

"Aliens are at 1800K now. They'll be here—"

Stan heard the sound of metal on metal, as if someone had just pounded the outer hull with a sledgehammer. Stan heard its reverberations even above the engine's whine.

Tag whirled in her seat, her eyes rolled up into the back of her head, interfacing with her neural. "Suggest an EM burst on the outer hull."

"That'll take all our electronics down until we can reboot—"

Andrada's voice was drowned out by the sound of a hundred sledgehammers. As if someone were building a railroad on the hull of the ship, metal struck metal all up and down the length of the ship, the blows coming more rapidly by the second. The din grew exponentially louder as thousands of creatures began pounding at the hull.

"Do it!" Santos shouted above the noise. "Full EM burst."

Tag squinted as she initiated the burst—and then Stan heard a pop.

The lights went out. His neural went offline. The whine of the engines disintegrated into silence. Stan felt a panicked vertigo as the artificial gravity cut out, leaving them floating blind and deaf in space.

"At least—" Andrade's voice began, but he was interrupted by the sound of metal pounding on metal once more.

CHAPTER ONE

Summoned. *It's never good news when you're summoned,* Jeff thought. Good news can be handled by neural. Performance reviews can be handled by neural. Mission assignments can be handled by neural. Only bad things have to be handled in person. They'd provided him with a very comfortable apartment, oppressively cheery in décor, specifically designed to offend few and please none. He hated it.

There were those who would say he hated everyone and everything, but they would be wrong. He would be the first to admit that he could be abrasive and anti-social, but he knew it was because he cared too much. He cared too much and had failed.

The call light blinked and the emitter directly below it chirped. "Showtime," he said aloud and permitted himself a groan as he stood and straightened his dress blues.

He touched the pad near the door and it slid open with a quiet pneumatic release. Captain Taylor stood just outside his door, more or less at parade rest.

"Jo," he said.

"Jeff," she said, turning briskly and power walking in the

direction of the space station's command center. He forced himself to keep up with her. "You cleaned up good," she said without looking at him.

He grunted. He liked Jo, more than he liked to admit. But they were both captains, and if anything, her ambition far exceeded his. There had been something between them once, but that was a long time ago. A part of him resented the situation, longed for things to be different, but he never blamed her.

It was kind of her to come for him—she could have sent a lackey.

"Where are we going?" he asked.

"Your orders were intentionally vague, so I hope you weren't obsessing over them. You're not in trouble or anything."

Jeff's eyebrows shot up. On the one hand, that was welcome news. On the other, the mystery just got deeper. "In that case, why not just handle this remotely?"

"How should I know? Maybe the admiral just likes to watch introverts squirm. Maybe it's a cruel streak. On the other hand…."

"What?"

"I had an uncle who was a monk, even a supermonk, you might say. A hermit. I don't mean it metaphorically, he was literally a hermit. Took vows and everything. Did you know that hermits are required to come together with their fellow monks once a day?"

"No."

"Neither did I. It avoids morbid isolation."

They walked down a long hall in uncomfortable silence.

"What are you trying to say, Jo?"

She got into an omnilift and only faced him when the door shut. In her own hard, angular way she was still pretty after all these years. "You can't punish yourself forever, Jeff."

He blinked but didn't answer her.

"Your isolation looks a lot like misanthropy, and it's being noticed."

"I thought you said this wasn't a dressing down."

"It isn't. But you're a hair's breadth from it. It's why I wanted to fetch you myself. Give you a heads-up. Warn you off before—"

"Before I cross the invisible line that separates pain-in-the-ass from liability?"

"That's less diplomatic than I would have said it, but sure."

"And this is you…taking me aside…as a friend?"

"As a colleague who respects you and doesn't want to see you wasting your potential." She rolled her eyes as the lift slowed to a stop. "Goddammit, yes! As a friend."

"Can you give me a heads-up what this is all about?"

"Not a chance, soldier."

They exited and Jeff noted they were outside the office of Admiral Paul Jennings.

"Jennings?"

"It's important, Jeff."

He whistled. The station housed a lot of the Colonial Defense Fleet's senior brass, but he hadn't expected to be summoned to the very top. "Why so hush-hush?"

"You'll find out soon enough."

"You sure there's nothing I need to know?"

"Relax. Just be yourself. On second thought, it would be a good idea to make eye contact and speak to people."

"Very funny."

"I *am* trying to help."

He knew that. He knew the complex political reality they

both lived in, all too well. He knew exactly in which ways her hands were tied. He knew how closely she could skirt the issue —whatever it was. She wasn't going to compromise herself for a moment, but she was still reaching out. "If I registered human emotion like a normal person, I'd be touched," he told her.

"I'll take that as a thank you."

"You do that." He tightened his jaw. The truth was, he *was* touched. It had been a long time since anyone had gone out on a limb for him. This wasn't exactly limb crawling, but it was *something*. To his surprise, he found he missed such somethings.

The door slid open and he heard Jennings' rough voice call, "Come!"

Jo gave him an "after you" motion with her hand.

"Huh," he said, and entered.

Admiral Jennings was standing at the ready, his hands behind his back, his face betraying nothing, except perhaps avuncular regard. A large round table took up most of the room, surrounded by stylish black chairs.

"Captain Bowers, thank you for coming," Jennings said.

He almost replied *'Didn't really have a choice'*, but thought better of it and simply nodded.

"That will be all, Captain Taylor."

Jo shot Jeff an encouraging glance and took her leave. Once the door had slid closed behind her, Admiral Jennings moved toward the wet bar. "I hear you two have history."

"A very short history," Bowers said. "We're both married to the CDF."

"You're not the only ones." Jennings poured himself a whiskey, and another for Bowers. He handed the glass to the captain.

"I don't really—"

"Yes, you do. You're going to need that, son."

It had been a very long time since Jeff had been called "son." Jeff accepted the glass and took a sip of the whiskey. It wasn't bad, which didn't surprise him, knowing what he did about the Admiral.

"You indicate in your file that you don't believe you are command material. But that's not what Admiral Tal or Colonel Mattocks or Captain Taylor or…God, anyone who has ever worked with you or commanded you says."

"Permission to speak freely, sir?"

Jennings waved his hand, as if batting protocol away like a pesky fly. "Of course."

"A man's own opinion of himself ought to be worth something."

"When you were on the Catskill operation, Captain, you made a judgment call in the field—one that any of us might have made in the same circumstances—*would have made,* most likely. It turned out to be the wrong call. That doesn't make you a bad commander."

"Is there anything else, sir?"

Jennings sighed and pulled up a star chart. It flickered in the air above the round meeting table, but quickly stabilized. Jeff walked toward it and within a few seconds got his bearings. "The Gliese system. That's where New Manila is," he said.

"Was."

Jeff's head jerked toward the Admiral. "Was?"

"We held the news of it back a cycle, but it's going to hit the feed very soon. They were expecting to make first contact."

"Sure. Can't access the feed and hear about anything else."

"As the aliens got closer, the Colony launched a reconnaissance ship. It was destroyed."

"Destroyed? How?"

"This is the only visual footage that we have." Jennings looked up, obviously triggering something in his neural. Jeff's own neural registered that it had received a packet. He accessed it. He closed his eyes in order to enter into the visual feed with as little distraction as possible. When it was over, he opened his eyes and clutched at the table for support.

"Sit down, son," Jennings said. He poured another slug into Jeff's glass. "And for God's sake, drink."

"How many ships?"

"One hundred and eleven verified. Probably more, though."

"And how many of these—"

"We're calling them the Prox."

"Why?"

"Because they were inbound from the general direction of Procyon—"

"Alpha Canis Minoris," Jeff said.

"That's the one. Now, we have no idea whether they're from a planet in the Procyon system or not—possibly they're from a planet *beyond* that system."

Jeff nodded. "How many of these were on each ship?"

"*On* is right. They appear to travel on the outside of the ships, not the inside. It looks like they've stripped the hulls completely off."

"That's not possible," Jeff said.

Jennings brought up a schematic of a CDF ship. "This is *The Envoy*, the ship that went to reconnoiter with the Prox. What you just saw in that file you watched were the Prox launching themselves from their own ship and propelling themselves—somehow—through the vacuum of space to attach themselves to *The Envoy*. The crew's feed indicates pounding on the hull until they punched through."

"And then?"

"Then we lost contact."

Jeff stared into his glass. "What do they want?"

"We don't know that."

"Are they intelligent?"

"They're piloting superluminal ships—or at least riding on them—so we have to assume so."

"And the colony?"

"They've gone completely dark. That's all we know."

"How many people are we talking about? I've never been to the New Manila Colony."

"The Filipinas Interplanetary Company says twelve million. Colonial Defense says more like nine."

Jeff nodded—it was the usual politics muddying the waters. The FIC wanted to maximize public perception of their loss; the CDF wanted to minimize panic.

Jeff looked up at Jennings. "This is above my clearance level."

"Not anymore. We need information—a lot more information than we have. We need someone to go out there and gather as much intel as possible without being detected."

"And that's where I come in."

"'Fraid so, son."

"What makes you think I won't get spotted?"

"Our best guess is that the Prox can detect energy—heat, radiation, electro—"

"I get it."

Jennings didn't seem to be put off, but instead took a seat near Jeff and continued without skipping a beat. "So we've got every engineer we can spare outfitting a Carson class scout ship with active camouflage, as well as heavy thermal and EM shielding."

"There's no way to completely shield anything," Jeff said.

"We know that," Jennings sighed. "We have no idea how sensitive their sensors—or senses—are. So...it's a risk." He looked up at Jeff apologetically. "We've plotted a course that will use the three suns of the Gliese system to block your approach to the outer system. Then you'll land on a large asteroid with an elliptical orbit that passes pretty close to New Manila Colony."

"How close?"

"127,000 kilometers."

Jeff whistled. "That's pretty close. Gotta seem like an occasional moon."

"The planet has a small moon already. But you're not wrong—they call the asteroid...*called* it *Pangalawang Buwan*—essentially, 'second moon.' We want you to land on the asteroid while it's at the far end of its orbit and let it act as a natural shield. You'll let it carry you toward the colony... and the Prox, of course."

"Why not send a probe?"

"Because we can't shut down a probe and get anything useful. It'll have to be 'on' and they'll see it."

"Got it. So I'm riding a dead ship planted on a careening asteroid hoping not to be eaten by bugs from somewhere beyond Procyon."

"That's the nutshell, yes."

"Do you have a duration estimate for this action?"

"It'll take you three months to get there at C5—"

"Which is the best a scout can do."

"Right. We've got a patch that might get C6 out of her, but it'll be unstable and should only be used in emergencies."

Jeff nodded, pulling up the Carson class schematics in his neural to do a quick check.

"But what's really going to seem like wasted time is hiding out on the asteroid waiting for its orbit to align with New Manila."

"How long?"

"We've worked it out to the second, but roughly six months."

Jeff nodded. "And three months back. We're talking about a year."

"If everything goes as planned, yes."

Jeff blinked and the schematics disappeared. He looked Jennings in the eye. "Is that why you're talking to *me*?"

"Is what why?" Jennings' brow furrowed.

"Admiral, let's not be polite. I know I have a reputation."

"There aren't many men we can send out on solo stretches like this without cracking. You seem to actually like it. Our psychologists say it's because of your own PTSD, and it isn't doing you any favors. But it's one of the things that make you valuable to us. Your battle scars, Captain, have turned out to be an asset."

"I won't let you down, sir." Jeff stood.

Jennings offered his hand. Jeff shook it.

"Admiral, if you don't mind, can I ask you a question?"

Jennings nodded.

"Taylor. She was the last person I was expecting to see. Since when is a captain acting as your errand boy?"

Jennings smiled but glanced away. "We want her close by because…well, she's our best chance of *handling* you."

"Thank you for your candor, but…am I really that difficult?"

"You said it yourself, Captain. You have a reputation."

THE JOURNEY out to New Manila had been uneventful, and he had passed the time studying the history and culture of the Filipino colony. He even had the synthesizer prepare him meals from the Filipino and the Asian fusion cuisine popular on the colony itself. If he was going to investigate something lost, a part of him felt obligated to understand exactly *what* had been lost.

The studying he had considered "work," but in his downtime he read a small stack of paperbacks, their papers yellowed and their covers worn, ripped, and sheathed in protective plastic. He'd picked them up—almost at random—at an antique stall on the Sol Command Station. He'd made a diverse selection: a Western adventure, two romance novels —one of them decidedly spicy—a spy thriller, and a dystopian novel geared for young adults—all from the mid-twenty-first century. He had read them all twice, and the spicy romance novel four times.

He was just at the point where Consuelo had told Geoff off for not respecting her profession and they'd had "angry sex"—one of his favorite parts of the novel—which did kind of disturb him when he stopped to think about it. But as the temperature fell, he pushed such self-examination away.

Despite the gravity of his mission, he enjoyed his time in space. In truth, something in his soul hungered for solitude, and in the nearly nine months since he had launched from Sol Station he had feasted well. His mind flashed back to when he was a teenager and had gotten lost in the woods around Anchorage. He was in the throes of hypothermia when his father had found him, and as he slowly warmed up in the back of the land rover, his father had given him a thorough tongue-lashing. "Why didn't you call for help?" his father had yelled. It was a good question. And the only answer that made sense was a fierce determination to find his way home on his own. *Is that pride?* he wondered. Maybe. But his father had just called it stupid. And when they had finally arrived home and got him into a warm tub, he saw that his father had been crying. Had he been crying the whole time he'd been yelling at him? Jeff didn't know, but he was too shocked to ask. "You've gotta let yourself be helped sometimes, Jeff," his father had said. He remembered thinking at the time, *Not if I can fucking help it.*

He smiled grimly at the memory, but felt a pang of guilt as he did so. His old man hadn't deserved that. Hell, no one had. Not Dad, not Jo, not anyone his obsessive need to do it himself had affected. And that obsession had just gotten worse since the Catskill incident.

As he had approached the Gliese 667 system almost six months ago, Jeff had powered down all engines and glided into a parallel path with the asteroid, then at the far end of its elliptical orbit. Within a few weeks, the paths converged, and using very few short bursts from the nav thrusters, Jeff guided the scout into a ravine on the asteroid that protected it from three of four sides, but left the viewing ports unobstructed. He extended the landing feet, inspired by those of a gecko, which gently reached out and gripped the asteroid, pulling the ship's belly tightly against the rock. Once the ship had "nested," its polymimetic skin changed texture and color to become indistinguishable from the rock it clung to. With a sigh he had switched off the main electricity panel. Only a highly shielded, isolated "box" continued to function, operating only the most basic life support functions.

The asteroid was tumbling slowly, completing a full rotation every twelve hours. While it was pointed away from the star Jeff, endured five hours of bitter cold, followed by an hour of mild, comfortable temperature as it rotated back into sight of Gliese 667. This was followed by five hours of oppressive heat, during which Jeff could do little but lounge, sweat, and read. Then another hour of productive respite, and back into the cold. Jeff wrapped himself in his blanket once more and waited.

After five and a half months of this, he was used to the routine. He made good use of his "spring" and "autumn" periods, as he often thought of them, searching out the remains of the New Manila colony, and watching for signs of Prox activity. Before launching, the station crew had added a high-power optical telescope. It was an archaic bit of technology, but once the scout ship powered down, it alone would allow Jeff to carry out his surveillance without detectable energy or heat signatures. Over the long weeks, as he got closer to the ruins of the colony, there had been much more to see. Jeff squinted into the telescope's eyepiece and turned the primitive knobs, adjusting its attitude.

He sighed and looked in the eyepiece again. As the asteroid drew nearer to the planet, he was beginning to see the devastation wrought by the Prox. He scratched out a few notes on a pad of paper with an old-fashioned lead pencil.

The files he'd reviewed on the colony had shown pristine cities, farms with thriving crops, and suburban areas with tree-lined streets. But all Jeff saw now as he tumbled within sight of the colony was rubble and the active and ongoing raping of the land and infrastructure. He gritted his teeth as he watched Prox tearing down entire skyscrapers and harvesting the wire and metal.

He had ceased to be angry—that had fueled him for a couple weeks. But now the anger had passed into a grim resolve for revenge. He felt calm as he contemplated it. It would be well planned, utterly devastating, as inevitable as carbon decay, and just as passionless. He knew these things with a certainty that was not rational, not emotional, just gut-solid true.

He adjusted the telescope using light micro-motions, refocusing on the space above the colony. He saw several ships careening stern over bow in their orbits, as lifeless as the castoff elytra of beetles. He ratcheted up the power on the 'scope and zeroed in on what was left of a massive battle cruiser, *The Empyrion*. He watched as Prox swarmed over it, ripping great sheets of metal from the hull. They reminded Jeff of enormous crabs, with squat, flat, armored bodies that moved sideways, and long, articulated tails that looked dangerously barbed at the tip.

As he watched, Jeff began to pick out different kinds of Prox, each of which seemed to have specialized functions. The largest he dubbed *soldiers*, harkening back to the various castes found in ant colonies. Each soldier was at least three meters across and about 1.75 meters high when their jittery legs were fully extended. Like living bulldozers, the soldiers used their huge claws to rip the hull plating off the ship as easily as opening a can of vegetables. Apparently they found it appetizing, as they often nibbled on it, eating the metal itself.

Workers were roughly a meter smaller widthwise than the soldiers. They had no tails, but had smaller, more intricate foreclaws. They flitted between the soldiers, sometimes crawling unnoticed on their flat backs, gathering up the weightless, tumbling sheets of reinforced steel with their numerous legs, all eight of which were moving in circles as if pedaling unseen bicycles. They hustled the plates off the ship, tumbling with them into space.

Every now and then a third class of Prox would approach the ship. They were smaller still, their foreclaws hardly differentiated from their other legs, their swimmeret tendrils extended, spiraling and coiling like a nest of great long snakes gathered in a bunch at their abdominal aprons. These wove around the hulls of the ruined ships, reaching out to touch—compulsively, it seemed to Jeff—every worker and soldier they passed. It looked as though they were delivering instructions, collecting progress reports and coordinating the frenetic activity. Jeff decided to call these *expediters.* "If they are distributing orders, where are they coming from?" Jeff's voiced seemed so loud in the solitude of the cabin that it startled even himself. He paused, scrawled some notes, and then flexed his writing hand against the rapidly accelerating chill. *Wintertime,* he thought. *Time to hang out with Toni.*

Jeff stowed the pad and pencil in a plastic pocket hanging from the telescope. Taking care not to bounce in the almost impossibly low gravity of the asteroid, he propelled himself hand-over-hand toward the stern of the ship, where the heat shield stored just a tiny bit more of the star's warmth than other parts of the hull.

Jeff was aware that this might also just be his imagination. He hadn't bothered to measure it, to see if it was actually true. It was the myth he told himself so that he would have reason to "migrate" to the stern. It was a routine, it kept him active. It was, in its own way, a liturgy of the hours, and he made a procession to his successive seasonal altars. The only thing he didn't do was pray. Instead, at this, his winter altar, he wrapped himself in his blanket and sat with his back against the heat shield. As the temperature cooled, he rocked back and forth to try to generate a little bit of warmth.

"Hey, Toni, did you fix your web?"

The CDF fleet was infested with spiders. It always had been, and although people frequently complained about them, for Jeff it was just a fact of life in space. G-forces, flightplan projections, radiation monitoring…and spiders. When people first went into space, no one had expected spiders to be a problem. No one had given them a second thought—just like they hadn't worried about koala or boa constrictor infestations. But there was something about space that drew them—something that allowed them to flourish here. It didn't matter how many times the maintenance crew fumigated a ship, the spiders would be back in force within just a few months. It was a mystery, but one which by now pretty much everyone accepted.

Jeff was glad of the company, although he didn't consciously admit this to himself. Most of the spiders were small, many were microscopic, but Toni was a rarity—a banded garden spider—large enough to have some personality and objectively beautiful with her brown and green zebra-like stripes running horizontally over her voluptuous abdomen.

During his last winter phase, Jeff had noticed that a couple of the strands of Toni's web had become unmoored, and the upper left section had been left waving in the low gravity. Such disrepair wasn't like Toni at all, who was never derelict about such things, and he expected to see the web once more in good repair. As he drew near he reached a hand out to grab a handle and slow himself down. Then he glanced at the web. The upper left section was still waving. He scowled in concern and moved in closer to the web, careful to stop himself before he plowed into it.

Toni was there, but instead of perching with her legs splayed out, confidently astride her silk, she was curled into a ball, held captive by her own web, as if she were prey. Her legs, once noble and slender, were tucked up under her body, the tips of them jutting out at odd angles, motionless and diminished.

Jeff's mouth was a grim line as he reached out a tentative finger and poked at her. She did not move. She was gone.

A pang of grief stabbed at his chest. Despite how expertly he had suppressed his emotions over the past several years, he still felt the sting of it. It seemed to him that the right thing to do was to simply *be* with her, as if sitting shiva. He stared at the husk of her and felt the prick of an emptiness that, had he allowed it, would have overwhelmed him much of the time.

His thoughts turned to Catskill. Normally, he was on guard against this. But Toni's death prised open a well-guarded door in his memory. He saw himself, as if at a distance, commanding his men. His friend Danny had been his second. They'd known each other since boot camp. They'd had a friendly rivalry since the day they'd met. And when Jeff had been tapped for command ahead of him, Danny had celebrated his promotion without a hint of wounded pride. He'd been a true friend until a hail of blaster fire had filled him with holes…until that day when every single crewmember under his command had been leveled, and Jeff had escaped only by being knocked unconscious and left for dead.

It was this that had led him to seek the solitude of deep space. There was no one to let down out here. There was no one to be responsible for. There was no one who might die should he go left when he should have gone right.

Jeff was so lost in his memories and grief that he didn't notice that his breath had turned frosty, or that his nose had begun to run, or that the blanket he pulled around himself was woefully inadequate. The air was growing warm again when an alarm sounded. It was a quiet alarm, but he heard the dissonant electronic tones as if they were blaring. He leaped up so fast he hit his head on the opposite side of the cabin before he could slow himself down. He cursed his carelessness, but with the help of the handles, found traction again and maneuvered to the shielded display. He tapped on the screen and found the source of it—proximity alert.

Jeff's heart jolted to twice its normal rate as he swung toward the telescope. He fixed his eye to the viewer and swept the sky for evidence of incoming Prox. The asteroid was still rotated away from the planet, so he couldn't see anything just yet. *Did they see me?* he wondered. *Have they detected my energy signature? I've been careful, and the tech crew was meticulous,* he reminded himself.

"Shit," he said aloud and slapped himself in the forehead. "I should have seen this." The asteroid was rich in various metals, but especially iron. Instantly, somehow, he knew. They hadn't seen *him*. They saw the asteroid. And it looked *tasty*. He was just a cherry riding on an irresistible sundae headed straight for the Prox's gaping mandibles.

"Dead meat," he said, because that's what he was. They were on their way toward the asteroid, and once they found *it*, they would inevitably find *him*. And *eat* him.

"Shit shit shit shit shit…" he repeated as he threw himself across the cabin toward the pilot's console. He snatched at an overhead handle and neatly swung into the command chair. If he hadn't been panicking he would have congratulated himself on such a gymnastic move, but all such thoughts were pushed well out of mind. His body automatically went through all the motions of his pre-flight checklist, while his mind raced through multiple aspects of his situation at once.

I can't outrun the fuckers, he thought. *Not in a scout. There's no way I can maintain the steady quantum field needed to go superluminal if I'm doing evasive maneuvers. Colony feed said the Prox were doing 1800K, but I can't do more than that under standard propulsion…* A monad of thought wondering at the impossibility of such a thing flitted into his consciousness, then out again. Despite the cold, he began to sweat as his thoughts flailed, looking for an out.

"Gravity assist," he said out loud. It was a long shot, but it was the only one he had.

He fired up his control panel, blinking as the lights flared on, the cabin filling with the humming of multiple systems stirring from sleep. He released and retracted the landing claws, leaving the scout floating free and beginning to drift from the surface of the asteroid.

His vision sparkled as his neural initialized, filling his field of view with diagnostics and informational displays. He used to take them for granted, but after living without them for so many months, they now felt like magic. He pulled up a virtual model of the system and asked the computer for a course that would give him maximum velocity in the shortest amount of time. Only one possibility resulted in survivable g-forces. He set his head firmly against the headrest and punched the engines for everything they had. The acceleration distorted his face as the scout's engine kicked away from the asteroid with explosive force. Jeff eased back as soon as he was clear, since he still had to be slow enough to maneuver.

He had the advantage of surprise, and he was determined to make the most of it. He could use the gravity of the asteroid—and at first that was his intention. But it would be far less help than the much denser planet beneath him. Surprise was surprise, and it wouldn't last long. He adjusted course and gunned it for the planet.

His slingshot course would use the massive gravity well of the planet to exponentially increase his velocity. By the time he reached the planet he could be doing nearly 700 kps. One orbit around the planet and he should be shooting off and away at nearly 20,000 kph, if he was lucky and the scout didn't shake apart.

Full sensors were up now, and information began pouring in simultaneously on his neural as well as the view pads in front of him. He did a sweep and found that the Prox that had been headed toward the asteroid had stopped and turned. Literally thousands, no, hundreds of thousands of Prox dismantling the colony and the other ships in orbit had also paused, as if momentarily frozen in time. *Probably awaiting orders*, Jeff thought. A moment later, they started moving —fast.

Jeff ran some intercept calculations—he'd have to dodge several of the Prox on the other side of the planet, and at his speed his maneuverability would be severely compromised. He fired up his defensive battery and prepped the particle cannons. If he couldn't go around them he would damn well blast *through* them. And there were a lot of them.

It doesn't matter, he told himself, his inner voice unreasonably calm and encouraging. *You'll make it or you won't. It's your best shot so go full out and fuck 'em 'til they take you down.*

He hit the 700K burst just at the apex of the gravity well. Within seconds he was going upwards of 12,000K and gaining every second. The burst was just icing on the cake.

He made sure his neural was interfacing properly with the weapons system, and, satisfied that it was, he released all the safeties, primed the particle cannons and tuned them to maximum force. Gripping the edges of his console, he closed his eyes and transferred his view to the outside visual array.

The ship was shuddering now under the gravitational grip of New Manila. It was literally being torn in two by tidal forces, twisting between the twin prongs of velocity and gravity. Jeff's mouth opened in a silent scream and his cheeks vibrated from the bodily drag. Jeff could feel his brain pressed painfully against the back of his skull. His speed was 18,000K as the ship began to emerge from the gravity well, hurled like an 80-ton stone from a sling toward the motionless stars.

The Prox were swarming him now. He was leaving thousands behind him in the dust, but those ahead of him were forming a gauntlet to block his escape. Flicking his eyes upward and to the left, he checked the power level on the weapons system and estimated he had about sixty particle blasts, more or less. He held off until he could see the articulated legs of the Prox directly ahead. Mere seconds from colliding with them, he lit them up with the particle cannon and saw their armored bodies explode outward in every direction. He felt the bump and scrape of their scattered parts bouncing off of his shields as their ship dove directly into his beams.

He pumped away at the cannon until he had cleared nine successive waves of Prox bodies, then a tenth. As he cleared the detritus of this final wave, he emerged into a clear field of stars. A sensor reminded him of the planet's moon dead ahead, and for a split second he deliberated. *Just head out into space and hope that it's enough?* he wondered, *Or slingshot off the moon as well?*

The moon as well, he decided. He plotted a second slingshot course, modulating his approach angle so that he'd be slung in the general direction of Sol, and of course, Earth.

He stopped noticing the shaking, until a panel rattled loose from the ceiling and gashed the side of his head. Blood streamed from his temple, and he wiped at it impatiently, trying to keep it out of his eyes. But mixed with the sweat, the blood seeped into his left eye despite his efforts. He squeezed that eye shut, and using a combination of neural and pad controls, braced himself for an acceleration that should exceed 32,000 kps. The ship's shaking became a shuddering again as the gravity began to tear at it. Jeff checked the proximity sensors and was relieved to see that the Prox were still a ways off. He was going to make it.

Hope and elation coursed through him as he prepared for the acceleration. He gripped the console again.

Just then an alarm began sounding. The notification in his neural identified the problem—maneuvering thrusters failure. He watched in horror as his escape trajectory faded and he saw the scout's icon circle the moon again and again and again, trapped now in a very fast orbit. Checking the proximity sensor, he saw the Prox closing in fast. He did a quick diagnostic on the maneuvering thrusters and felt his stomach sink into his boots as he saw the entire starboard array missing.

Is there any point in landing on the moon? His mind raced. *Is it rock or metal? Is it made of anything the Prox would find desirable?* He could do a mineralogical investigation, but he didn't have time for that now. The fact that the Prox were not already consuming it gave him hope. He only had to find a place to hide on the blind side of the moon.

First things first, he told himself. Using his remaining thrusters, he did the one thing they would permit—flip over. He entered his intentions into the neural and let it make the calculations. Then he just held on as the flight action played itself out. He felt the quick jerk of the thrusters, too quick for vertigo, then felt the ship punch forward as the stern thruster array lit up for one more all-out burn. He watched his speed plummet until it was within safety range for a landing—but only just.

Landing with only port thrusters was going to be a challenge. Not impossible, but deep in a crevasse of his brain that he actively suppressed, he knew that it was very, very unlikely. With one eye on his altitude, he searched frantically for a place to hide. His hopes leaped as he saw a canyon about 2,000 kilometers dead ahead. He entered the coordinates as his destination, and the scout spun as he tried to even out its landing.

Descending now, Jeff's eyebrows bunched in confusion as he saw the lunar landscape. It was red. He shook his head and, adjusting the outboard sensor array with his neural, he looked again. It was as if he were looking at Earth's moon through a crimson filter. *Must be damage to the sensor array from the shaking*, he thought. Somehow the green and blue rods must have gotten fried, and he was only receiving input from the red rods. *That must be it,* he thought.

As the ground got closer, Jeff saw that it wasn't just the rocks he was seeing, but some kind of crystalline structure covering every surface. It sparkled in the starlight as the scout hurled past it, but before Jeff could question what it was he was seeing, metal collided with rock and the scout began to tumble end over end. Everything went black as Jeff felt himself spinning in the night for what seemed an eternity. Then with a final screech of tearing metal, the ship lurched to a stop.

Jeff's pinprick of consciousness was snuffed out in the vacuum.

CHAPTER TWO

They're eating my brain, was Jeff's first conscious thought, after...after what? The images cascaded over him in waves. He saw scenes from childhood, the husk of Toni, her legs tucked up beneath her, the night nearly two decades ago when Jo had stumbled into his bed, drunk. He saw his own flight from the Prox, the heat of battle in which he saw the entire platoon under his command obliterated before his eyes in explosive bursts of gore, the lunar surface rushing up under his scout at a lethal velocity.

He opened his eyes—at least he had the impulse to open his eyes, and there was a corresponding visual result. He did not, however, seem to actually have a body. Or, if he did have a body, he was not receiving any sensations from it. He seemed to be floating in deep space, although there were no planets or stars. The only thing he could see looked like...*Like what?* he wondered. *Fireflies,* he decided. *They look just like swarms of fireflies...little blue fireflies.*

I crashed, he thought. No one could have survived an impact with the lunar surface at that speed. The uneven surface would have ripped right through any deflectors or grav-repelling fields the scout had been outfitted with. There was no way...and yet, how was he thinking? How was he conscious? *I'm dead,* he thought.

Yes, dead. It was another voice, not his own. It seemed to be coming from within his own head, though—his own, nonexistent head. *But also, not dead.*

Some of the fireflies seemed to migrate toward one another, hovering before his (impossible but seemingly present) field of vision. Jeff felt a sensation flow over his nonexistent body—as if someone were pouring warm liquid over his head and neck. More of the fireflies flew in from somewhere, until there were millions of them, swarming, bunching, congealing into something larger, denser. The mass of fireflies took on the vague shape of a person—a person of light. He?...she?...shone with an almost impossible luminosity, yet it was not painful to look at it—indeed he did not know how to look away. The person's outline was blurry, but it slowly gained definition, even as the brightness dimmed. It resolved into a solid person of flesh and blood. A person Jeff recognized.

Danny? Jeff thought.

Danny smiled. But Danny was dead. Danny's spine had been ripped out by a particle cannon. *Yes, Danny,* the voice in his head said. Danny's lips moved to form the words, but the sound did not come from his direction. In fact, there was no sound, just...meaning. *But also, not Danny. We perceive that your consciousness is more likely to be receptive to a human form. If we appeared as we are, you would not recognize us as...sentient. We have borrowed this pattern from your memories. We hope it is not unpleasant.* Danny smiled. The look on his face was compassionate and encouraging.

No...just a shock.

We could choose another, Danny said. He became fuzzy around the edges.

No, it's fine. Just...give me a second.

Danny resolved again, his face patient and kind. Danny had been both of those things, but he had also been tough and sardonic. There was no hint of those qualities in this Danny.

Is incorporeality upsetting for you?

It's...unsettling, Jeff responded.

Please forgive our insensitivity, Danny's voice said in his head.

Another constellation of fireflies swarmed into his vision, but instead of coalescing into a form he could see, they seemed to somehow coalesce into a form he inhabited. He looked down—for suddenly there seemed to be a *down*—and saw a body of light forming around his consciousness. A luminescent hand waved before his vision, and he was waving it. Legs spiraled as if he were riding a bicycle, but then found footing as a surface coalesced beneath him.

The light body was now a body of flesh, but it did not feel like his old body. It *teemed*—as if he were amped on the kind of uppers they gave out to rouse slow-run colonists from hybersleep. But it did seem solid, as did the floor, as did Danny. Around them, though, seemed to be a lot of white... nothing. The whiteness just faded into infinity on all sides, creating a ghostly, fog-like effect that was disorienting.

"Um...could we have some walls, please?" Jeff spoke out loud.

"Of course. Forgive us."

Again, he felt warmth flowing down the back of his neck. The whiteness took on color and texture. Patterns emerged and when everything stopped whirling, Jeff instantly recognized his family's hunting lodge near Anchorage. He could think of no more peaceful or pleasant place.

"Will this suffice?"

"This is...wonderful." He was surprised at how much more safe he felt, how much he craved being *bounded*. He would not have guessed it.

"So this is my family's lodge, but where are we *really*?"

Danny's face tightened up into a smile. "We are *inside*."

"Inside what?"

"Inside us." Danny's tone indicated that this was self-evident.

"I'm sorry," Jeff shook his head. "I need more...I don't understand."

"We are the Ulim. We are inside our mind."

"Our mind? As in, yours and mine?"

"There is no yours. Only ours."

"Can you...explain?"

Danny's smile faded into a look of tolerant patience, as one might have with an annoyingly curious child.

"We are the Ulim. We were once as humans are. We had bodies, although they were much different from yours. Over many millennia we learned to create."

"Do you mean that you learned to make art?"

"No, I mean that we learned to create life. We learned how to pull it apart and put it back together. We learned how to rearrange matter at will at the molecular level. We learned to weave it from the dead elements around us. We learned how to make it sentient, and how to transfer sentience."

Jeff cocked his head. "So what happened to you?"

Danny held his hands out, palms up. "We ascended."

"What does that mean, *ascended*?"

"We mapped our patterns. We created a...system...that we could live in. Then we entered it."

"A system?"

"Yes." Danny closed his eyes and seemed to be searching

for a word. "I am reviewing your pattern.... A program. We entered the program."

"Like a computer program?"

"Yes, but not mechanical. Biological."

Jeff's eyes snapped open wide. "The red moss on the moon's surface. That's not moss, is it?"

"No. It is a sentient crystalline matrix. It covers the moon. It feeds on starlight. It needs little maintenance. It is our home. It is where our pattern resides. We live...within. We are there now. *You* are there. Here." He smiled, apparently at the awkwardness of language.

"Is there only one...Ulim?" Jeff asked.

"Yes, there is only one Ulim, but we are numerous. We are on this world, and many others. We can choose to separate out patterns—"

"Partition," Jeff suggested.

"Yes, if you like. We can choose to merge as well. You are separated from the main body of the Ulim."

"Why, is...? Oh. Quarantine."

"Just so, yes. There is a lot of pain in your pattern. Pain that would prove...toxic to us."

"That...makes a hell of a lot of sense."

"We are pleased that you do not take offense."

"I crashed on your...on the moon. Did I hurt anyone? I'm sure I damaged the red...the crystal formations."

"All that we are is endlessly redundant. No pattern is destroyed if the host is destroyed. And the host has repaired itself. All is well. Be at peace."

Jeff breathed a deep sigh of relief. He looked down at his hands. They were, in fact, *his* hands. He even saw the scar from the time he had cut his finger as a boy. "So I'm dead. I'm...what? A ghost?"

"No, not a ghost. You are a living pattern, just as we are.

We have joined your pattern to ours. You are in us and we are in you. We are one being. And we live forever. As long as you are united to us, *you* will live forever."

"But I *did* die."

"What you once were is gone, that is true. And yet you *are*. This is something to be glad of, yes?" There was a hint of Danny's old buck-up cheerfulness in the voice. Jeff wasn't fooled by it, but he welcomed it.

A fearful thought struck him. "I'm trapped here, aren't I?" The crystalline "moss" might sustain his consciousness, but was it really living or just surviving? He suddenly felt claustrophobic.

"No. You are not. We can delete your pattern. You can *choose* to die."

"I can't stay in this...this *state* forever," he waved at the hunting lodge. As comforting as it was, he knew it was an illusion. It was an emotionally pleasant prison, but... no more. "I would go crazy. I...I don't mean to sound ungrateful, but the truth is that I'd *rather* die."

"We have had much debate over your future—the *if* of your future, to be exact."

"And what did you decide?" If there was one thing Jeff hated more than anything else, it was being at someone's mercy.

"Some have argued that deleting your pattern is best, but this is not our way." He smiled compassionately. "Coercion is not our way. The consensus is that you must be given a choice."

"So...what are my options?" He had the distinct feeling of waiting for the other shoe to drop.

"You can stay here, or we can reconstitute you in your accustomed form. We can return you to your home. It is... what we would want, if the situation were reversed."

"That's very Golden Rule of you," Jeff said, smiling. "But...that's impossible. My ship was destroyed."

"Yes. That is a problem. We did not capture the pattern of your ship in any way that could be understood or retained. Your ship has no pattern remaining, no DNA, no memories. Nothing but a tangle of elements, which we have absorbed."

"And no blueprints."

"Precisely. We do have your memories of the vessel, but they are mere impressions, neither complete nor precise enough to reconstitute the vessel. Nor can we simply coalesce you on the moon."

"I would die instantly."

"Not instantly. Quickly."

"Horribly," Jeff whispered.

"We do not choose this."

"We are in agreement on this." Jeff mimicked Pseudo-Danny's clipped, patient tone. Pseudo-Danny didn't seem to notice. "We are going to return you your planet of origin—to Earth."

Jeff's eyebrows bunched in confusion. "You just said yourself that my ship was destroyed. How do you intend to *get* me to Earth?"

"We will simply reconstitute you on Earth."

"Simply? You make it sound like you're going down to the corner store for the paper."

Jeff watched Danny's eyes move back and forth as he searched for the references. He must have found them, because he smiled. "It is actually easier than that. We don't have to put on our slippers."

"How could it possibly be easy? We're 24 light years from there."

"As I have said, we have Ulim on many worlds. We did

not travel there in ships, crossing the distance in-between. We simply *shifted* there."

"Shifted?"

Danny renewed his "patient" smile. At least it seemed genuine. "Space is malleable. Distance is illusory. If you understand that, you can take this point here," Danny held one hand up, as if he were pinching a point in space and holding it between his thumb and forefinger, "and bring it together with this point here." He pinched a different point about two feet away from the first. Then he brought the pinched fingers together, forming for a moment the infinity sign from the two circles made by the fingers of his two hands. He unpinched his fingers, releasing whatever fabric of space they held. "Simple."

"Is this some form of technology?" Jeff asked.

"At first it was. Not now. Now it is merely…knowing how to do it. At first it seemed like a trick. Later we realized it was simply how things worked."

"Didn't you need to know how it worked in order to do it at the beginning?"

"Yes, but we did not have the strength of mind to put it into effect. We needed…technological assistance. Later, we did not."

"So you can…shift…to any point in the universe at will, using the power of your mind?"

"We can."

"And that is how you'll return me to earth?"

"It is. If you choose to go. You may stay here, if you like." He gestured at the hunting lodge again.

"You know the answer to that."

"We do."

Jeff stood up and began pacing, stroking his chin. "You said my body was destroyed."

"It was disassembled, but we recorded its pattern as it did so."

"And you'll reassemble me on Earth?"

"Not from the same matter. We will reassemble your pattern from matter we take from the environment of Earth."

"Then it won't really be me, will it?"

Danny looked confused. "The pattern will be identical."

"It will look and sound like me. But I'm dead. My body is gone."

"Your consciousness remains. Your body will be as it was before. All that you were, you will be again. There will be no loss and no change; continuity will be maintained. Any other distinction is meaningless."

"There are many among my people who would argue that point with you."

"They will not have the opportunity."

"So, you're asking me to return home and to pretend like nothing happened?"

"We are not asking you to pretend at all. Tell them what happened to you. We ask for no secrecy, no allegiance."

Jeff nodded, taking this in. He had to admit, if they were telling him the truth about everything, then the Ulim were nothing if not honorable. "I don't mind being dead," Jeff said, finally. "In a way, it's what I signed up for. It's the acceptable risk, you know? And even if you said, 'We're going to wipe your pattern now,' I would have no reason to complain. Having this little chat with you…it's a form of mercy, even if it was the last thing I ever did. And I would be fine with that. I really would be. I really…*am*."

Jeff continued to pace as he thought. Danny waited patiently, not at all uncomfortable with the silence. That suited Jeff just fine. He was used to silence.

"Will I feel this…fucking great all the time?" he held his

hand up. "Don't answer that. It doesn't matter. The thing is, I'll be different. Myself, and not myself."

"You are beginning to sound like us," Danny grinned.

Jeff nodded. "You know, if it meant just my death, I wouldn't complain. But it's more than that now. I *know* things…things that could save lives." His head snapped up. "Okay. I don't know what life in this new body you promise will be like, but I have a duty to perform. So…I accept. I want to live."

Before he could take another breath the floor disappeared from beneath him, and the walls faded out. Once more Jeff felt himself suspended in space, surrounded by the little blue fireflies. Jeff reached out his hand to touch them, then realized he had no hand. Were these fireflies real, then? He doubted it. He suspected they were being offered to him as a gift—as a symbol or metaphor for something real but incorporeal. But a symbol for what?

For them, he thought to himself. *Each of these fireflies is an Ulim.* He knew it was true. He felt the "rightness" of it. They were nodes of consciousness. Then they began to change. The thrill of wonder rolled over him as he watched each node blossom—opening like a flower, gossamer tendrils reaching out to connect with their neighbors, until all were joined in an immense network. Then, in a single collective motion, each node turned its bloom toward the triple stars of Gliese 667. As they absorbed the power from the suns, a thrumming began. It sounded like an electronic signal, but it also sounded like a tribal rhythm. It pulsed.

What am I seeing? Jeff wondered. The nodes were aligning themselves with the star, capturing as much of its radiation, its energy as they could. They were sending that energy somewhere, for some purpose, but for what?

He realized that he, too, was a node. There were parts of

him that were connected, and parts that only he had access to. They knew their "partition" business very well. But he was blossoming. He was collecting energy. He was sending it. He was *them*. He was One and Many. He was conscious of a small "him" and a large "him." The small him was vulnerable, a mixture of hope and aspiration and pain. He pitied it. The large Him was infinite, confident, purposeful.

The large Him reached out, and with unseen hands gripped two very distant corners of space. He began to pull, and he felt the fabric of the distance field give—at first reluctantly, then more easily, until the whole stretch of it was pliable, shapable. He was conscious of every millimeter of that distance field—every asteroid, every star, every planet, every pocket of gas, every particle of dust. It was all known and comprehended.

Then, as if fingers had suddenly set a globe spinning—a globe that he was standing on—Jeff felt a jarring shift in perspective. It was disorienting, but not unpleasant. And he realized that it was no longer Gliese 518 before him, but the familiar yellow glow of Sol. And there, at no distance at all, spun a blue green planet that he knew was Home.

Emotion swelled within him, and he felt a sympathetic echo from the other nodes. They seemed...*happy* for him. No. It was the feeling he had when he finished painting a wall or completing a report. A job well done. It was *satisfaction*.

The earth was rushing toward him now. He saw the familiar continents, then the contours of countries—the verdancy of Greenland, Canada, Russia, and Alaska, the desert wastes of Europe, the States and China...and the radioactive husk of Australia. He saw himself rushing toward Anchorage, toward the tower that housed his apartment.

The partition opened, and Jeff had the distinct and uncomfortable sensation of being fully known. He was being read. An itching began on his scalp—*the scalp I do not have*, he reminded himself—and then spread. Like a wildfire, it raged over his head, down his neck, over his chest, down his arms. Jeff opened his mouth to scream—and actually screamed. And screamed. And screamed.

The pain was like nothing he had ever experienced before. It was as if every cell in his body was being torched simultaneously. He blazed, he swelled, he ground his teeth and wondered that they could be ground. And then the fire cooled. He felt the soft breeze of the air conditioner tingle on his skin, felt the trembling of the hair on his arm.

He had eyes. He opened them. He saw nothing. No, there, a tiny orange light. A node? No, it couldn't be. It wasn't blue, for one thing.

He had ears. He listened. He heard a heartbeat, not his own. Mechanical. A toc-toc-toc sound, almost too loud to be real. *Dad's clock,* he thought. He had fallen asleep to that sound most of his adult life. It was a mantel clock his father had inherited from a distant relative and passed along to Jeff when he graduated from the Academy.

But that wasn't possible. That clock was twenty-four light years away. But the sound was old. Familiar. It sounded like Comfort.

He turned over, feeling the cool fabric of the sheet against his cheek. He had a cheek. He had an arm. He reached it out, the motions familiar from thousands of repetitions over many years. He found the light switch. He turned it on.

He blinked with the force of it. His vision was blurry at first, but it was clear what he was seeing. He was in his bedroom in Anchorage, in his own apartment. He swung his legs out of bed. They looked just like his legs. He stood. They held him.

It was his body, and it was not his body. It looked and

acted like his own, but it thrummed with life in a way his old body hadn't since he had been young. He felt the back of the couch. It seemed real. The clock was on the mantel, louder than ever.

It has to be an illusion, he thought, *just like the hunting lodge.* He reached out with his mind to commune with the other nodes, but he found none. He was alone.

Then his ears were assaulted by the sound of a crash. Military police burst through the door, weapons poised and the yelling of many voices. Not comprehending, Jeff stared at them until they tackled him. He laid face down on the floor, felt the intrusion of a blue-uniformed knee pressing painfully into his fresh new spine, did not resist as they cuffed his hands.

CHAPTER THREE

Dr. Emma Stewart sighed as she resumed her seat. First she'd gotten up because the room was too cold. Then she needed "new" tea, because the old tea no longer tasted right. Eventually she realized that she was just procrastinating. There would always be something else that needed doing, anything but what she *needed* to do. And what she *needed* to do was to make a decision.

Two files were open in the air reader before her. Two faces hovering over her desk projecting fresh-faced enthusiasm, straight out of the Colonial Science Corps Academy. One male, one female. Both *summa cum laude*, one year apart. Both had written fascinating dissertations. But she only needed one quantum seismologist for the new team she was building. Debby was a dog person, did watercolor in her spare time, unmarried. Ulrich was a cat person, shot skeet, gay, married with one girl. Debby seemed by-the-book, worked well in an authority structure. She had done a two-year turn in the Colonial Defense Fleet, honorably discharged with commendations. Ulrich was out-of-the-box, arrested twice for protesting CDF military actions. Both were brilliant.

And here she was, about to make a decision that would change the trajectory of their lives forever. She was usually good at decisions, but this was two people's lives she was going to impact—and their families. If one of them were clearly better suited, it would be one thing, but—

An alert in her neural lit up. She looked up, blinked, and read the message.

—Need you for a consult ASAP. C-378.

She scowled. Since when did Admiral Jennings need her input on anything? She closed the air reader and the two faces cascaded into the quartz desktop. The C-300 block was...she stood up. Psychological holding. She shook her head. She could be remembering that wrong. She looked up and consulted her neural. No, that was correct. How could she possibly help with a psych eval? She was a physicist.

In point of fact, she was the CSC's chief physicist and the ranking scientist on Sol Station. Jennings knew her time was valuable, and he had never charged her with anything frivolous before. She fought a wave of resentment. Then the thought emerged: *There is tea to get.* She deflated. Who was she fooling? She wasn't getting anything done here. She rose, put on a sweater, and headed for the hall.

———

IT TOOK her fifteen minutes to navigate from the main science block to psych services. Something about the distance between them comforted her. *There should be a great distance, after all, between real science and*—she stopped herself before she could complete the unkind thought. She'd dated a psychologist once. Benjamin. That had ended with her kicking him in the teeth. She did *not* like to be pathologized, and his nightly diagnoses of her complex neuroses went from cute to infuriating pretty quickly. She let a wave of rage surge through her, then subside.

She punched the blinking access square just outside of C-378 and the door slid open. Stepping inside, she gave a quick nod to Admiral Jennings, who was seated at a consult table. Another CDF officer was with him. She didn't know her, but she read her rank. Captain. And too pretty by half. Emma hated her already.

"Ah, Dr. Stewart. Thank you for coming so quickly," Jennings said, standing briefly. "Please join us. Do you know Captain Jo Taylor?"

"No. Nice to meet you," Emma offered her hand and a half-smile. Taylor half-rose, shook it, and returned to her seat.

"What's up? You know things are—"

"Hectic, I imagine. How's that new team coming?"

"Almost together. Two more and we'll have a full complement. Then it'll just be support personnel, but I can delegate that."

"I should think so," Jennings' mouth quirked. He wasn't at all interested in her team, but the man had a sense of decorum. He also knew that he wasn't her boss, and he needed to play nice. And Emma knew that nothing on the station happened without his approval. Her world, she mused, was a bureaucratic and diplomatic ball of tangled yarn.

Jennings pointed at the far wall. Emma took a seat to the Admiral's right and looked at the wall. It faded into video feed from an evaluation room. In it was a man dressed in standard CDF casuals. His hair was longer than regulation. He needed a shave. His eyes stared into space as if he were deep in thought. They were eyes that were quick with intelligence, but dark with…what? Guilt? He scratched the back of his neck.

The door slid open and a man walked in, dressed in

medical whites. He was tall and lean, with a whisper of a mustache on his upper lip. "Ted," Emma blurted out, "what are—"

"Dr. Osprey is a psychiatrist," Jennings said.

"Yes, I…we know each other," Emma said. Ted had been Benjamin's best friend on the station, and probably still was. His eyes danced knowingly over her, then moved on to Captain Taylor.

Once the introductions had been made, Jennings pointed at the patient. "Captain Jeff Bowers. We sent him out on a reconnaissance mission nine months ago."

"Where?" Osprey asked.

"Now, you all have clearance, and I'm invoking it now," Jennings shifted uncomfortably in his seat. He looked up and blinked, calling up a file on his neural. A 3-D image hovered above the table. "This is where the New Manila colony used to be," he said, "until alien hostiles we're calling the Prox destroyed it. That much is common knowledge. Now we get classified: We didn't get much info on them before the station went dark, so we sent Captain Bowers to gather intelligence. And, unfortunately, his ship was destroyed."

"How?" Emma asked.

"Crashed on New Manila's moon," Captain Taylor said.

"New Manila is how many light years away?" Emma asked.

"Twenty-four," Jennings answered.

"What did the moon base say?" Emma asked.

"What moon base?" Jennings returned.

"The New Manila moon base."

"There is no New Manila moon base."

Emma blinked. "Then his ship can't have been badly damaged."

"According to Captain Bowers, it was completely destroyed," Jo responded.

"This moon has breathable atmosphere, then. How—"

"No. There's no atmosphere to speak of."

"Then...who rescued him?"

"That's why you're here, Doctor," Jennings said. "Just... let's let the man speak for himself."

The far wall shuddered and resolved into feed of what looked like a CDF interrogation. Captain Bowers was there, in the same clothes, looking exactly the same. His voice was reedy and uncertain as he spoke. He told his story, from leaving Sol station to waking up in his apartment in Anchorage. The feed shuddered again and they were once more looking at live feed of the captain staring into space.

"I need to know what really happened," Jennings said. "You're my team. I want you all to put everything aside and give this top priority. Captain Taylor, that's an order. Doctors...this is an urgent request."

Emma nodded. Well, she'd been looking for a distraction. *Careful what you wish for,* she thought to herself.

Jennings rose and started pacing. Emma thought his uniform looked a bit too tight on his boxy, sedentary frame. "The way I see it, we've got three possibilities." He looked up and accessed something on his neural. Then, as he spoke, bullet points appeared on the far wall next to the feed of Jeff. "Option one, he's telling the truth. Option two, he never left in the first place and he somehow tricked all of us with simulated information. Or option three, he's not really Captain Bowers."

"You mean, like an android?" Emma asked. "Surely that's easy to rule out."

"We have." Doctor Osprey pulled up a file and projected it over the table. "He's a completely normal human. He still has every childhood scar, every mole and dimple. His DNA is an exact match, right down to the radiation damage from his duty in the nebula. His neural implants have complete records, going all the way back to when they were first installed. Even the serial numbers are correct."

"And psychologically?" Emma asked.

Osprey's eyebrows rose, acknowledging the question. "Psychologically he's...fragile. But he's *himself*. His personality profile is an exact match to the last time we tested him. He knows things that only Captain Bowers could know."

"And how could *you* know that?" Emma asked.

"How much technical detail do you want me to go into?" He gave her an imperious sneer.

"Do you two have anything going on between you I need to know about?" Jennings asked.

"We know each other." Emma said. "Not well."

"I want professionals on this case. If I see another flash of personal animosity like that one, Doctor Osprey, we'll find ourselves another doctor."

"I understand," Osprey said, looking down.

"Are you finished?" Jennings asked.

"No. There's...one more thing."

"What's that?" Jennings asked.

"He's too young."

"What?" Emma asked. "What do you mean?"

"This guy is in his mid-fifties. His metabolism should be slowing down. His glandulars ought to be congruent with his age, but they aren't. He's running the glandulars of a twenty-year-old. All of his vitals, in fact—they're the vitals of a kid straight out of boot camp. So...I think there's some veracity to your option number three, Admiral. This isn't the same Jeff Bowers that left."

"Which means he could be telling the truth," Captain

Taylor said, a note of hope in her voice. "He said that his body was destroyed and he was reconstituted here by the... what did he call them?"

"The Ulim," Jennings offered. "So how do we know he isn't an Ulim plant? Or a Prox plant for that matter? Maybe Captain Bowers is telling us what he thinks is the truth, but he's been duped by the very alien bastards we sent him out there to spy on."

Jo whistled. "When you put it like that, it...well, it doesn't sound implausible. And if the Prox can duplicate people down to that level of detail..."

"There will be no fighting them," Jennings admitted. "Let's pray that is not the case. Doctor Osprey, I want you to head up a medical team that will put Captain Bowers through every test known to humanity—both medical and psychological. Hell, enlist a witch doctor if it will rule anything out. I want to know *exactly* what happened to him."

"What about option number two?" Emma asked. "How sure are you that he actually went out there?"

Jennings pulled up flight plans, with dated transponder signals that were clearly indicated by flashing green lights. "All of our data is here, Doctor Stewart. I hope you'll review it carefully. But...I think you'll find what we found. Every transponder node hit just on the second it should have. No hidden carrier waves, no encrypted virus sequences, no indication of any possible way he could have tripped them remotely. That particular scout hit every one of those destination markers, and I've got a whole operations team who will say the same. What's more, we have medical readings on his vitals for every second of his trip—not a blip, not a dead space, not a single moment that caused us any concern or question. Everything is recorded, right down to his occasional ventricular arrhythmia. The medical team is just as certain—

he was *out there*." Jennings leaned on the table, both fists planted solidly on its quartz top. "I want you to prove them wrong, Doctor. If there's a hole in this, I want you to find it."

"I'll do my best, sir."

"Thank you." He rose and rubbed at his eyes.

"And then there's option one," Jo said, her arms crossed over her dress blues.

"And then there's option one," Jennings agreed. "The problem with option one, though, is that it's impossible."

"No. It's improbable," Jo said. "That's not the same thing. I agree that the age hiccup is a problem. But if he's telling the truth, that would account for it, wouldn't it? His...pattern, as he called it, it would have been him through and through, right down to his implants. But when they were re-created—"

"If they were recreated," Jennings corrected.

"If they were recreated, then everything would be new. The stress of age wouldn't apply. Doesn't that speak in *favor* of his story?"

Osprey nodded, looking distantly off into space.

"As for option two, if you find that he really *did* go, then it's impossible that he could be back. Unless, again, he's telling the truth."

It was Emma's turn to nod.

"Or unless he's a Prox plant," Jennings said.

"Didn't he bring back intelligence on the Prox?" Jo asked.

"Yes, but how do we know he's not just telling us what they want us to hear?" Jennings asked.

"He's not lying," Osprey said. "I can tell you that for sure. Even if what he's saying isn't what happened, he is convinced that it is."

"I want to talk to him," Jo said.

"You're the one who..." Osprey began, but then stopped, obviously trying to find a delicate way to put things.

"I'm the one he has an emotional connection to," Jo said. Her face was rigid, but her feelings were betrayed by a flush of red rising into her cheeks.

Osprey looked at Jennings. "It's a good idea. He might open up to her. And psychologically, he needs…well, maybe not her, but he needs some substantial human contact."

Jennings nodded. "All right. We have our work cut out for us. Doctors, I am grateful for your assistance. And spare no expense—the full resources of the CDF are at your disposal for this." He jerked his head toward the door. "Captain Taylor, with me."

———————————   ·

ADMIRAL JENNINGS WAVED Captain Taylor into the medical exam room. Protocol dictated that he should enter first, but there was a vestige of chivalry in him that overrode even military training. She considered taking offense at the sexist act but decided there were more important things afoot. "Thank you," she said instead. The door closed behind them, and Jo unconsciously glanced at the place in the wall where the cameras were hidden, through which Doctors Stewart and Osprey were watching them.

And then there was Jeff in front of her. Big, tough Jeff, whom she had loved once upon a time, now looking diminished and haggard. He saw them and rose unsteadily, saluting. Bags hung under his eyes and his color was pale. "As you were," Jennings said. Jeff sunk back down to his seat.

"You hungry?" Jo asked, taking a seat across the table from him. Jennings took the seat beside her.

"I could eat," Jeff answered.

"I'll bet you could eat a horse by now," she said, and looked back up at the camera. "Can you guys order him some food?" It was silly to pretend no one was watching, after all. Jeff knew the score. "He hates tomatoes."

Jeff grinned at her sideways. "Thanks."

"You could have asked for it yourself."

"I've been kinda busy."

"You get probed and prodded this much, you've earned some chow, soldier," Jennings said.

"Yes, sir," Jeff said.

"I'm sorry for all the tests and interviews."

"No need, Admiral. It's protocol. It has to be done. I don't resent it. It's important."

"I'm glad you feel that way," Jennings nodded. He folded his hands on the table in front of him and cocked his head. "Captain Bowers, are you *you*?"

Jo was surprised at the brevity and directness of the question.

"I am," Jeff answered. "And I'm not."

"Can you explain that?"

"I really am me. I'm the same guy who launched nine months ago. I'm the same guy who rode that asteroid in. The same guy who crash-landed on that moon. I have...continuity of consciousness. But this body..." he shook his head. "It's new."

"Son, you have the same scars you've had since you were a boy," Jennings contradicted him.

"It's a good copy, that's for sure," Jeff agreed. "But it's still a copy."

"Son, if that's the case, I'm having a hard time figuring out how I can ask the CDF to trust you."

"If I were them...I *wouldn't* trust me," Jeff shook his head gravely. "Not for a second."

"Should *I* trust you?" Jennings asked.

"As much as you ever did, I guess," Jeff answered. "Different body. Still a prick, though. I can tell you that for certain."

Jennings smiled at that and pulled at his face. "Okay. I want to hear it again. All of it. From the top."

Jeff nodded, knowing the drill, and launched into the story again. This time he added details, thoughts, feelings, intuitions, impressions. Jo saw him grasping at anything new. It was clear to her that he was giving them 110% percent. He was cooperating, and then some. When he was done, Jennings asked him to do it again. He didn't balk, he didn't complain. He just launched right in.

Halfway through the second telling of the session, kitchen staff brought in a hot meal. Jeff fell onto it like a man whose parachute wouldn't open. Jo had never seen anyone demolish a plate of turkey and stuffing that fast. He even seemed a little winded as he forked the last bite into his mouth.

"You could've taken your time with that," Jennings said.

"I could have, but didn't," Jeff said, his mouth still full. "Where was I?"

He didn't pick up mid-sentence, but he might as well have. When he was done, Jennings leaned on his elbows. "Back up to the Ulim. Where are they from?"

Jeff looked up, thinking. "I don't know that, sir. If I sink into the memory of being…connected to them, I can see constellations, but I don't recognize them. And I'm sorry to say that in the moment, I didn't think to ask."

Jennings looked at his hands, nodding thoughtfully. "I don't blame you, son. How many of them are there?"

"They are many…and one." Jeff flinched. "Sorry. That's how they talk. I seem to have picked it up. There are millions of nodes—maybe billions, spread out over more star systems than I could count—but it's kind of a hive mind. There's no individual locus of consciousness, not that I could tell." He leaned back. "They can isolate consciousness. Like, they can wall it off, like they did me at first, for their own protection. But it's not their normal state."

"Do you know anything about their evolution?" Jo asked.

"Only that they used to be like us—not humanoid, maybe, but individual creatures, flesh and blood. Their current form is synthetic, not organic."

"They *made* it? They made *themselves*?" Jennings asked.

"Yes, I suppose they must have. They made it, then they transferred their consciousness into it."

"The Noosphere," Jo whispered.

"What?" Jennings asked.

"A 20th-century theory of the future evolution of humankind. Turned out not to be true for us—at least not yet. But maybe for them…" she bit her finger thoughtfully.

"What do they want with us?" Jennings asked.

Jeff shrugged. "Nothing, so far as I could tell."

"What do you mean, *nothing*?"

"I think they're aware of us. But I don't think we're more than a blip on their radar screen. They don't seem to be concerned about us. They don't seem to want anything from us. They pretty much just ignore us."

"Then why didn't they just ignore you?" Jennings' eyebrows bunched in confusion.

"I think because they took pity on me." Jeff looked the old man in the eye. "That's what happened, sir. They felt sorry for me and they saved me. It was an act of mercy. They don't have any designs on us. There's nothing they want from us. Other than to just be left alone, I guess."

"Then why were they there on that moon?"

Jeff shook his head. "Maybe they were there before we ever landed on New Manila. Maybe *we're* the interlopers. Maybe they only shifted there after the Prox attack—maybe they're worried about the Prox and *they're studying them, too*." Jeff suddenly sat up, and Jo imagined his vitals surging from his excitement.

"But you don't know that," Jennings said.

"No sir." Jeff slumped in his chair again. He yawned.

Jennings' head jerked up and Jo watched as he retrieved something from his neural. "Got a medical report back. No trace of nanotechnology—the kind that would be necessary to reconstruct you."

Jeff shrugged. "I guess they don't use nanobots. What about crystalline structures?"

Jennings shook his head. "It doesn't say."

Jeff tsked.

Jo placed her palms down on the cool surface of the table-top. "I want to hear how you got back here again."

Jeff nodded. "Okay. I saw this…it was like a cartoon in my head…of alien flowers turning toward the sun."

"A cartoon?" Jo asked.

"Yes."

"What did it mean?"

"I think it was an artistic representation of what was really happening."

"Do you mean like a dream is often a symbolic represen-tation of all that's going on in your life at the moment?" Jo asked.

Jeff moved his head from side to side. "Kind of, I guess. Not so abstract. More…representational. There weren't really flowers, but the Ulim were doing what flowers do, and for the same reason."

"To glean energy?" Jennings asked.

"Yes."

"Then what, son?"

"It's hard to say…I just have flashes…impressions."

Jennings leaned back. "Captain, do you mind if we mine those impressions?"

"What do you mean?"

"I mean, we get a little assistance in here and yank those memories out by the roots."

Jeff nodded. "Be my guest."

"Osprey, you're on," Jennings said to the room. A few minutes later, Doctor Osprey entered with a tray in hand. He stood by the table awkwardly.

Jeff rose, a bit unsteadily, and offered his hand. "Anyone gonna stick a probe in my behind better be on a first-name basis."

Osprey shook it, the corners of a smile turning up on his lips. "No anal probes. I promise."

"What does a guy have to do to get a good anal probe around here?" Jeff sat back down.

Jo snickered and patted his beefy hand, noting how delicate and small her own was in comparison.

Doctor Osprey pulled out the chair next to Jeff and picked a pneumosyringe out of the tray. He checked its settings and then set it against Jeff's throat. "This won't sting."

"Wouldn't matter if it did."

There was a quiet burst of air, and Jeff's eyelids began to flutter. Osprey turned his head and plugged a neural stimulator into his netpiece. It began to blink. "As soon as his eyes close, you can start asking him."

"I didn't want him asleep, goddam it," Jennings barked.

"Don't worry. Ascleperine is a hypnotic, not a narcotic. It won't make him sleepy, just introverted. And the neural stimulator will make sure he stays awake."

Jeff's eyelids finally rested on his sunken cheeks. "Okay. Ask away."

Jennings looked dubious, so Jo took the lead. "Jeff, tell us how you got from the New Manila moon to your bedroom in Anchorage."

"The nodes were winking at me...like fireflies. Then they turned and faced the sun...drinking it up, drinking it up." His words were slurred, but easily understandable. "So many Ulim, all iskondica for the trajj."

"All what for the what?" Jennings asked.

"Then I was with all the trajj, all the way to the top. I could see everything they saw. I could feel it. All of it. Impejaktallic, if you know what I mean."

Jennings looked at Jo and squeezed his hands together, eyes wide. "I'm not sure I do, son."

Then Jeff held his hands out, feeling at the space in front of him as if searching for invisible pull-tabs. "We reached out with our ulnic durr and grabbed the stellak jnar and the stellak ifna." He was talking faster now, clearly excited. A look of fresh wonder broke out over his face. His eyes were still closed, but he held his countenance up toward the light. "And then we pulled." He was hyperventilating now.

Jo looked at Osprey and mouthed, "Is he okay?"

Osprey nodded confidently. Then Jo's hair started to float. So did the doctor's. The cords to the neural stimulator rose as well, as if the gravity generator had gone out and they were suddenly drifting in free space.

"What the fuck?" Jennings asked.

"More tzzen, oppenco tzzen," Jeff said, his mouth starting to foam up. "Ah! There! Yes!" he shouted, a huge smile breaking out on his face. The overhead lights dimmed, as if someone had just turned down a rheostat. "That's it. Afinjjad!"

Jo felt the floor buck beneath her, felt her stomach rise up in protest. She was dizzy with sudden vertigo. Jeff started bleating—not like a goat, but like some unholy mixture of despair and pain and surprise.

Then he stopped. Her hair fell. The lights came back on. Jeff's body was slumped over the table. And on the table—

"Dear God," Jennings said, and clutched at the framed portrait. He dropped the picture just as fast, staring at his hands.

"What is it?" Jo asked reflexively.

"It's burning hot," he said. He held his hands in front of him like a doctor after scrubbing for surgery. But he looked past them to the portrait, lying askew on the table. "That's my wife and son," Jennings nodded. He locked eyes with Jo. "I keep that in my office."

———

"DID THAT…JUST HAPPEN?" Jo asked no one in particular. Jennings felt paralyzed and said nothing. Osprey, however, didn't suffer from the same paralysis. He jumped up and felt for a pulse at Jeff's neck. Apparently satisfied, Jennings saw him look up and blink, no doubt accessing the captain's vitals.

"Is he okay?" Jo asked.

"He'll live. But let's get him to the infirmary to do a full workup. Whatever he just did here…I don't think the human body was designed to do." Jennings saw Osprey's eyes darting back and forth, navigating menus and no doubt putting in an emergency call.

A red light appeared in the Admiral's peripheral vision. He jerked up and cocked his head, retrieving the message. Then he turned to Jo. "Captain, I…I'm needed elsewhere."

"Something wrong, Admiral?"

"I can't tell you that yet. Stay with him, will you? Send me updates, even if I don't respond."

"Of course."

With stiff movements, Jennings rose and strode out of the interrogation room.

As he walked, the Admiral quickly fired off a message of his own.

—I want the full report. Now.

A moment later, the response pinged in his left eye.

—We're still waiting for it. Sending you everything we've got.

—SAR

Send as received. Jennings had a reputation as a hard ass —fair, but a hard ass just the same. But he knew he didn't hold a candle to his personal secretary, Lieutenant Liu. Adrian was the most no-nonsense person Jennings had ever met, and Jennings trusted him completely. If Adrian got even a scrap of intelligence, Jennings knew he would receive it.

It took five minutes to navigate to his office. As the door slid open Lieutenant Liu snapped to attention. "As you were," Jennings said, striding toward his desk. "What do you have?"

"Incoming signal from the CDF station *Buckland* on the ansible...playable...*now*."

A hologram shimmered in the space just in front of Jennings' desk, showing a star field with a looming planet in the upper right. "That's not *Buckland*," Jennings said.

"I wouldn't know sir."

There was a crackle, and Jennings heard a voice. "CSC station *Buckland* here, Dr. Talon Burton sending. We received this transmission from the merchant vessel *Arcadia*. It wasn't coded to trigger the autorepeater and there's no intended recipient. It's kind of the video equivalent of a scream in the dark. We thought the CDF ought to see it."

"See what?" Jennings said to the room. And then he saw it.

He skirted his desk and came closer to the hologram. He knew if he got too close to it the resolution would deteriorate, so he hovered to find the optimal distance. "Prox," he said. The shape of the ship was unmistakable. A moment later, he saw a second ship emerge from behind the planet. Then a third. "Christ," he swore. "Any way to contact the *Arcadia*?"

"No sir. This is it."

Jennings felt a cold chill spread from his neck down his back as he watched scores of the Prox disengage from their ship and fly directly toward him, toward the camera, toward the *Arcadia*. Jennings expected to feel the impact of the first of the creatures as it lit upon the ship, but the camera didn't even shake. And of course there was no sound. There was just a long shot of enemy creature after enemy creature flying past the camera, until the transmission went black.

"Exactly where was the *Arcadia* located?"

A star chart sprung up in the air where the transmission had been moments before. A red dot indicated the *Arcadia*'s last known location. "Was the *Arcadia* closer to Earth than New Manila or farther away?"

"Closer, sir. If you were to draw a straight line from New Manila to Earth, you'd pass right through that spot."

"I was afraid you'd say that. Lieutenant, what is between *that spot* and Earth?"

"You want a list?"

"Yes, I want a goddam list."

"I'll send it to your neural, sir."

Jennings sighed. "I'm sorry, Adrian. I'm just..."

"I get it sir. No need. You should have the file now."

Jennings pulled it up and whistled. There were about fifty inhabited projects—from colonies to space stations to mining operations to transport and merchant vessels. All were moving targets, of course, but for the moment, all of them fell roughly on a line from the *Arcadia*'s last known position and the Sol system.

"The next sizable colony in its path—"

"Deseret Colony, sir."

"The Mormons."

"Yes sir."

"Distance?"

"Seventeen light years."

"Based on what we know about the cruising speed of the Prox—"

"That's almost nothing, sir."

"Well, how long would it take us at top speed to cross that distance?"

"About fourteen days, sir."

Jennings looked down. "Open a real-time ansible channel to CDF HQ in Regina, as well as our bases on Mars and Europa."

"Yes sir."

"We need every available ship with more than a pop-gun aboard *en route* to Deseret yesterday," he said. "And we need to alert the colony as well, have them muster everything they can."

"They have a formidable defense force, sir."

"Good to hear it. Tell them to get everything they've got in the air."

"Yes sir."

"Oh, and Lieutenant, while we're at it, we might as well remind the Mormons to pray."

EMMA STEWART PAUSED at the door. "Is it okay to come in?" she asked.

Captain Taylor waved her in. "Thanks for coming."

"I'm not a medical doctor, you know," she said.

"No...we're well supplied with those here. That's not why I requested you."

"You think I have some explanation for what happened in there?" Emma took a seat on the other side of Jeff's bed.

"I'm hoping you have a theory," Jo confessed. "Rumor has it you're the best theoretical physicist we have."

"I'm flattered, but they're called 'rumors' for a reason." Captain Taylor was still too pretty, but Emma was warming up to her. Her devotion to Captain Bowers was plain.

Just then Jeff began to stir. He stretched his legs and curled onto his side. Then he must have realized he wasn't alone because he sprung up into a sitting position and looked around wildly.

"Whoa there, soldier," Captain Taylor said with a wry smile. "At ease."

Jeff sank back down on the pillow. Jo hit a button on the bed frame and it rose into a sitting position. "Thanks," Jeff said.

Just then a nurse rushed in, his dreadlocks flailing. "Is he awake?"

"He's awake."

The nurse studied his vitals on the wall display. He keyed in an IV drip adjustment, then turned to Jeff. "How are you feeling?"

"Like I was hit with a landspeeder. I wasn't, right?"

"No landspeeders on the station, no."

"That rules out that theory."

"You were just dehydrated. And exhausted. You need fluids and rest."

"I need to get back to work."

"You *need* a jigsaw puzzle."

Jeff scowled at him. Captain Taylor and Dr. Stewart waited until the nurse finished his business. As soon as he was out of the room, both turned their eyes to Jeff.

"Okay, Captain, how did you do that?" Emma asked.

"Do what?" Jeff asked.

Jo took his hand and smiled encouragingly. "Do you remember…transporting the picture frame from the Admiral's office?"

Jeff cocked his head. Then he found the memory. He brightened a bit. "Oh yeah…that was weird."

Emma tried not to laugh. "That's one way of putting it."

Jeff smiled at her.

"So, tell us how, Jeff," Jo said, squeezing his hand.

"I'm not sure I can explain that, because I don't know."

"We're asking the wrong question, then," Emma said. "Let's try this: Tell us about the *experience* of moving the picture. What do you remember? What were your thoughts and feelings? Physical sensations?"

"Oh, okay. That I can do." Jeff bit his lip, remembering. "It's not like a conscious memory, though. It's more like trying to grasp at a dream. It's…wispy."

"Grab all you can, then," Jo encouraged him.

"I remember how I felt when I was…you know…I was one being, with the Ulim. I remember what it was like to be them, how they reached out—" he closed his eyes and felt at the air with outstretched arms, "how they grabbed it—"

"Grabbed what?" Emma asked.

"Grabbed…space, I guess. So, I just did it again. I was able to find that same place in my head…you know, where they did it…and I was able to do it, too."

"Take us step-by-step," Emma said.

"Okay, sure. I…uh…I closed my eyes, and I felt the big space."

"Big space?" Emma asked.

"Yeah. Oceanic. Infinite. I was able to see…to be…everything. Then I reached out and grabbed it."

"Space?"

"Yes. But it wasn't working. And I realized it was because I have so little power. You know, just what my mitochondria are generating. It's…well, it's not a lot. I needed more—a lot more."

"So what did you do?" Emma asked.

"I did what the Ulim did. I saw myself twisting toward the light, then opening like a flower—"

"You opened like a flower?" Jo asked incredulously.

Emma shot her a warning look. Jo slunk a bit in her seat.

"Yeah, that's what it was like. I felt the power, from the lights—"

"That's not a lot of power, either, those are LQDs."

"It was enough," Jeff said, his eyes still closed. Emma could tell he was concentrating on vividly reliving the experience. "I reached out to the lights and…absorbed the energy. I directed it into my fingers—"

"Your real fingers?" Emma asked.

"Uh…no. The fingers in my mind. Sorry, I know how that sounds."

"Keep going, soldier," Jo said.

"I felt it running through me, the energy," he said, his face brightening, as if he were feeling that energy again. "Then… it was strange. I didn't just feel like I was one with everything. I could actually *see* everything. I could see through the walls. I could see the Ulim on the New Manila moon. I could see every person, every creature on every world…kind of all at once. Distance…there wasn't any distance. You know how it's always *now*? Every *place* was *here*." He opened his eyes and stared at the hands in front of him. "Here," he repeated.

"The picture?" Emma prompted.

"Oh. Yeah. The energy was beginning to…well, the energy wasn't giving out, but I was…I don't know how to put this. My ability to channel it was flagging. I got really tired really fast. So I just grabbed the space around a random object—something nearby, something I knew would have some meaning."

"That's good, Captain," Emma said. "Just stay with the memories a little bit longer. When you grabbed the space around the picture, how did you *move* it?"

"I…uh…" Jeff rubbed his head. Then he closed his eyes again and reached his fingers out as far as they could go. He mimed grabbing at something, pinching the air between his thumbs and forefingers. "I just…*squashed* the space between the photo and the table we were sitting at."

"You *squashed* the space?" Jo asked, frowning.

"Yeah, like pushing the space between them out of the way until the picture and the desk were in the same spot, you know, physically. I gripped the space around the photo, and then I just let go. I guess I released the pressure I'd built up and it snapped back, kind of like a rubber band or a spring being released. And once I did that, all the…distance rushed back in—"

"But the picture remained on this side of the distance gap." Emma looked away as she spoke, thinking.

"Yeah. That's it exactly," Jeff agreed.

Emma nodded. "It sounds like your perception went four-dimensional."

Jeff cocked an eyebrow. "I thought the fourth dimension was time."

She shook her head. "That's different. Space actually has

a fourth physical dimension, at right angles to the three we perceive normally—that is, width, height and depth."

"Superluminal travel is only possible because of the fourth dimension," Jo added.

"Yes." Emma pointed at Jo. "A quantum engine warps three-space in the fourth dimension, compressing it in front of a ship, expanding it behind. And the ship surfs that wave in a bubble of normal, unwarped space."

Jeff stared at her, blinking.

"Okay, let's take it down a level," Emma suggested. "There was a book written in 1884 called *Flatland*, and it tried to help people visualize the fourth dimension. A map is flat, right? It's two-dimensional. If your whole world was inside the map, your line of sight would stop at the first object that was in your way. But an observer in three-space would be able to see the entire map at once. You'd be able to see over any two-dimensional obstacles, even *inside* objects."

Jo nodded. "You'd also be able to pick the map up and fold it so that any two points were next to each other."

"Exactly!" Emma said, a broad smile breaking out on her face. "So, what if that's what Jeff was able to do, only in three-dimensional space? What if he tapped into the fourth dimension where he was able to see every point at once?"

"A circle whose center is everywhere and whose circumference is nowhere," Jo recited.

"Huh? What was that?" Emma asked, cocking her head.

"Just…something I read somewhere. I think it's Meister Eckhart."

Jeff nodded. "Well, that's not far off, I think. But the thing about your analogy is that if you're looking down at the map, then you're also outside of the map. I didn't feel like I was outside the universe. Just…present at every point in it."

"It's an analogy," Emma waved his objection away. "You can't drive it to Toledo."

"Where the fuck is Toledo?" Jo asked.

"It used to be in the old sunbelt," Jeff said. "It got scorched, of course."

Jo shifted in her seat. "Jeff, do you think you could do this again? The frame trick, I mean."

Jeff nodded. "Yeah, I don't see why not. I can't do it right now, though. I'm pretty beat."

Emma frowned, staring at a blank space on the wall. "Do you think you could move something...larger?"

Jeff shrugged. "Sure. The only thing I'm not sure about is the energy. I mean, I used the energy from the lights this time, and I think the picture frame was...small. Commensurate, I guess you could say, to the amount of energy I was able to draw. If I wanted to move something larger, then I think I'd need more energy."

"But you don't know," Emma said. It wasn't a question. "So let's find out."

———

JENNINGS HAD WORKED through the night and had mobilized everything possible. Every ship at his disposal was being prepped and staffed at that very moment. The first of them would launch in just under two hours, and he had only one more appointment to make. He looked around his office and noted for the first time how spare and sterile it was. What was he trying to save, after all, if not life and beauty and art? And yet he had no time for such things in his own life, had devoted no wall space to them. His office had all the charm of an industrial storage room. Becky, if she were still living, would never have permitted this. She would have breezed in one day when he was out and made the place human. Livable. Homey, even. She wouldn't have asked permission. That wasn't her way. She would have just done it. Perhaps that's why he hadn't. There was no way he could have done it as good as she would have.

But he could just hear her clicking her tongue at him, looking at this place. He looked up and made a note on his neural.

—Potted plant. Landscape.

Becky wasn't partial to landscapes, but he liked them. In his mind's eye he saw an oil painting of a windswept Scottish shoreline, perhaps something from the 19th century. He was no great expert on art, but the image in his mind was so vivid he was sure it must exist somewhere. And finding it might make an excellent diversion once he was planetside. For now, though, there were lives to save. He looked up and sent a message to Liu.

—Do you have those time estimates?

A few moments later the answer came.

—Just in. You're not going to like them. If we launch according to schedule, the first of our warships will arrive about eight hours after the Prox do.

"Shit," Jennings said, and punched at the arm of his chair.

—We have to get them there faster.

—Not possible, sir. That estimate is based on a cruising speed of C8.

Dammit, he didn't want those ships there in fifteen days, he wanted them there *now*. He wanted… His eyes rested on the negative space left where the picture of Becky and their kids had been "jumped" from. He usually felt a slight ache when he looked at that picture. He wasn't prepared for a deeper ache now that it was gone.

—Keep me apprised.

He leaped up and began speed walking toward the infirmary. Along the way he sent messages to Captain Taylor and Dr. Stewart, asking them to assemble and give him a full report. Ten minutes later he arrived at the door to Jeff's room. Dr. Stewart arrived a minute later. Jo wasn't far behind. "I don't suggest we go in," Emma said.

"Because?"

"Because he's sleeping. The…squashing…takes a lot out of him. He needs to rest."

"Squashing? Is that what we're calling it?"

"It's what he called it. It's not a technical term, I'll give you that. But until we know what he's actually doing, there *isn't* a technical term for it." Emma waved her arm down the hall. "There's a consult room nearby. Let's go there."

Jennings and Jo followed her down a corridor and into a soft-lit room with a few comfortable chairs gathered around a holodisplay. Jennings sat on the edge of one of the chairs. He turned to Jo. "How do you think he's holding up…I mean, emotionally?"

Jo shrugged. "It's hard to tell with Jeff. He's not exactly a guy who wears his heart on his sleeve. He seems fine to me, though. I mean, I'm not Doctor Osprey, but he seems pretty normal, actually. He's not traumatized or anything. He's certainly cooperating."

Jennings pursed his lips and nodded.

"Admiral, can I ask you something?" Jo asked. "Do you…believe him?"

"Captain Bowers? You mean, do I believe he's telling the truth?" Jennings looked her in the eye. "Hell yes, I believe him. I still have a lot of questions, but my gut knows the truth of it. He's the same man I sent out there. And no one could… no one can do what he did earlier today. No one. He doesn't have any more clue than we do what happened there, I'm sure of that."

He turned to Emma. "I want to find out how he did that. More than that, I want to know how we can *use* it."

"Use it?" Emma frowned.

"Doctor, we have a classified situation going on right now. I can't tell you any details, but what I can say is that people are going to die because we can't get to them in time. If we can figure out how he does…what he does…" he didn't finish the sentence. He stared at the floor, at the worn seam of his boot.

"I get it," Emma said. "We're going to need a lab."

"We're going to need a place where no one will ask any goddam questions," Jennings said. "If word got out about this…let's just say I wouldn't want to…lose control of our asset."

"Jeff's an asset?" Jo asked, a dark note in her voice.

"My God, Captain, I hope so." Jennings made for the door. "And Captain," he paused, "I need to see you in my office in five minutes. You might want to…hell, you might want to say goodbye."

JO STEPPED IN, looking apprehensive. "What did you want to see me about, sir?" The door slid shut behind her.

Jennings sighed. He called up the cartography holo and waved at it. "The Prox are approaching Deseret Colony. They'll arrive in eleven days."

Jo nodded. She didn't look the slightest bit surprised. Or scared. She just looked *determined*. That was good. "I know you want to be here for Captain Bowers right now, but—"

"Permission to speak freely, sir?"

"Of course."

"I want to be wherever you think I can do the most good. Yes, I have…I care about Captain Bowers. But if I were going to let that get in the way of my duty I would have married him fifteen years ago. I didn't and I don't regret it. You put me where you need me."

"That's what I like about you, Jo. Brassier balls than a monkey. Here's the problem, our fleet can't get there for eleven days, and that's all out at C8."

Jo's eyes moved back and forth as she thought. "What kind of defenses do—"

"Considerable, thank God. More than New Manila had. But will it be enough? I've got scientists from all over the world giving me conflicting opinions about that. The problem is that we know so little about the Prox. If we could capture one of them, we could study it, figure out its limitations. But for now, that's way down on my to-do list."

"What's at the top, sir?"

"Blowing them out of the fucking sky."

"I'm your man, sir," Jo said.

"I hope so, Captain, because I'm giving you the only ship that has a chance of making it there before the Prox do. The *Essex* is the prototype for the Victory class of warships. It's untried in battle, but it's ready to go. It will also get you C8.4."

Jo's eyes widened. She was no dummy. She knew that C-velocity was exponential rather than incremental. She'd be there ahead of the Prox. Not by much, but by God, she'd make it.

"Firepower, sir?" she asked.

"Sixty-eight point-adjustable particle cannons aft and fore, four sear-laser ports with 360-degree targetability, five hundred two cloaked torpedoes, both forty and sixty megaton."

Jo whistled. "I could do some serious damage with that, sir."

"I'm counting on it." Jennings looked up and checked the time on his neural. "Gather your duffle. You launch in twenty minutes."

CHAPTER FOUR

"Welcome to Alberta, Captain." A young enlisted woman moved to hoist Jeff's duffle from the shuttle. Jeff stepped in front of her and lifted it out himself.

"Nobody's entirely welcome in Alberta," he said. "And I'll carry my own bag, thank you."

"Yes sir," the private avoided looking him in the eye.

A moment later Doctor Stewart was beside him. "Why is no one entirely welcome in Alberta?" she asked.

"Oh. Uh…hi." Jeff considered apologizing for his surliness, but thought better of it. He offered his hand, and Emma shook it. He was a little unsettled by her. She wasn't quite his type—a little too overtly feminine. But there was something about her that made him forget his shoe size momentarily whenever he was around her. Instead of looking at her, Jeff deliberately looked around, noting the prairie filled with wild grasses and flowers, underneath the biggest sky he ever remembered seeing.

"Thank you, private," Emma said, dismissing the young woman. "C'mon, Captain, let's get you settled in." With a jerk of her head, she set out for the few structures marring the landscape. "Are you feeling better?"

"It's good to be on terra firma."

"Hmm…" Emma narrowed her eyes at him as he fell into pace beside her. "Nice dodge. I'll have to be careful of that. But I thought you didn't mind being in space?"

"I don't. That doesn't mean I don't like being planetside. Besides, there are fewer spiders here."

Emma laughed. "You got me there. Christ, the spiders."

"So what do we have here?" Jeff gestured at the buildings.

Emma indicated an old farmhouse that looked like it was straight out of a postcard. "The house is HQ here. The longhouses behind are barracks. You get a private room in the house."

"You're shitting me. Why?"

"The gossip is that it's because you're a lucky bastard and for some reason Jennings thinks it's important that you rest."

"No complaints here."

"Next to the longhouses are the mess and rec hall."

"How many stationed here?"

"It's pretty much a skeleton crew," Emma said. "And as I'm sure you've guessed, this is top secret."

"I'm good with that." Jeff gave a quick nod. "What's with the big place?" He indicated with his chin a large, prefabricated box of a building to the left of the barracks.

"Half of that is our lab."

"And the other half?"

"The most powerful electrical generator on the hemisphere."

"What? Why?"

"Because you'll need it." Emma stopped and looked puzzled. "At least, that's what you suggested."

"No, I mean why is there a massive electrical generator out here...in the middle of a cornfield? Why isn't it powering a city?"

"Oh," Emma resumed her pace. "We had limited choices, really. Most generators are...well, *they're near cities.*"

"I'm not an idiot," Jeff complained. "My question was about *this* generator and why it's *not* near a city."

"I know you're not, Captain. But the answer to your question is, I'm afraid, above both of our security clearances."

"Like fuck it is."

"So you *are* feeling better," Emma grinned.

"What makes you say that?"

"Everyone says that you're normally a son of a bitch."

Jeff grunted, but couldn't help smiling. "Okay, I can see it. Jennings picked this site because it's nearly deserted. If we blow anything up—"

"Who would know?" Emma finished his sentence. "I mean, besides the mallards?"

───────────

JO LOOKED up and accessed her neural. Reports from all over the ship were coming in like clockwork, exactly as they should. None were marked urgent, but she scanned them anyway. Everything seemed ship-shape except for a malfunctioning food synthesizer unit in the aft mess.

She ran her fingers over the arm of the command chair, feeling once again the thrill of being at the helm of such an impressive vessel. Everything about the *Essex* gleamed. The stars on the viewscreen looked immobile, but she knew that was just an illusion, like staring at the hands of an old-fashioned clock. They were moving, just too slowly to see. And yet, she felt she could *almost* see them moving. After all, she had never gone this fast before. No humans ever had. It seemed incredible that she didn't feel like she was moving at all.

She rose and did a lap around the bridge, looking over the shoulders of her bridge crew, as if making sure all was in order. Commander Fin, her navigator, looked over at her as she approached him, and gave her a patient smile. She avoided going too close, not wanting to annoy him.

Her crew was not battle-tested, and that concerned her. They had nearly two weeks in space without much to do, and she wanted to make good use of that time. Starting tomorrow they'd be running emergency drills and battle scenarios.

The lift door hissed open and Commander Tohi entered. He had been assigned to be her number one, her second in command. Captains usually chose their own number ones, but time had not afforded her that luxury. She'd met the Pacific Islander only briefly since their launch, and he seemed a surly fellow. Her gut told her that he had a chip on his shoulder about something, but she would need to have a sit-down with him to figure out what. Well, it wasn't like they didn't have time. "Report, Mr. Tohi?"

The Commander went to the spare duty station without answering, turning his back on her. Jo felt the hair rise on her neck, and she looked around at her bridge crew to gauge their reactions to this unprovoked insubordination. Commander Fin's spine straightened and he studiously kept his eyes fixed on the panel in front of him. To his left, Lieutenant Frey froze, her hands poised over her communications panel. Her eyes darted back and forth, trying not to react to the fact that the captain was looking at her. To Fin's right, Weaponer Raj turned and, unfazed and unafraid, glanced back and forth between the captain and Commander Tohi, a look of puzzlement on his face. Chief

Engineer Laru raised one eyebrow but otherwise appeared impassive.

Jo hated confrontations like these. But they were, unfortunately, part of the job. She drew a deep breath and stood, stepping off of the command podium and taking the few steps over to the duty station. "Mr. Tohi," she said.

His face was buried in a monitor and he did not look up. "I'm listening," he said.

"Mr. Tohi, you are in imminent danger of losing your commission if you don't forget about the fascinating object on your viewscreen this moment and face your commanding officer."

Mr. Tohi looked up then, his face a hard mask of resentment and anger.

"Mr. Tohi, do we have a problem?"

"The only problem, sir, is that I have been prepping this ship for the past nine months. I know her inside and out."

"And you think the conn should be yours."

"It should be. And everyone here thinks so."

Jo looked around at the bridge crew again. Everyone was looking at them now. When she met his eye, Fin looked away.

"Weaponer Raj, do you think Commander Tohi ought to be captain?"

Raj looked back and forth between them some more before answering. Finally he spoke, his words careful and deliberate. "I think Commander Tohi has done a fine job preparing this ship. I think he is untested in battle."

"And what is your opinion of me, Weaponer?"

"I do not know you, sir. But your war record is...impressive, sir."

"Will you have any hesitation about following me into battle, Mr. Raj?"

"None whatsoever, Captain."

"You will let me buy you a drink after your bridge shift, Weaponer."

"Yes, sir."

"Mr. Tohi, whose decision was it to put me in charge of the *Essex*?"

"Admiral Jennings."

Jo noted he omitted the "sir" he owed her. He would pay for that.

"And are you in the habit of second-guessing Admiral Jennings?"

Tohi didn't answer, but she could see his quick eyes darting back and forth as he thought about it.

"Commander Fin, please pull up star chart 47392-E and display it on the forward viewscreen."

"Yes sir."

"Commander Tohi, please join me. I want to show you something." She stepped away from the duty station and down two steps to the broad space in front of the viewscreen. She didn't need to look over her shoulder to know what Tohi was doing. He was sitting straight up in his chair, looking at the accusing eyes of the bridge crew. Slowly, he'd rise to his feet, extricate himself from the duty station, and step down.

She heard his foot on the carpeted stair and knew she was right. She continued staring up at the star chart calmly, her hands behind her back. A few moments later, Tohi was standing beside her.

"Yes?" he asked. Not "yes, sir," she noted.

"Being a battle commander requires seeing what's coming, even when it's invisible," she said to him, her voice patient and kind, as if talking to a child. Her tone was perfectly calculated to piss him off.

"If you look there," she pointed at a star cluster in the Horsehead Nebula. "What *can't* you see?"

Tohi squinted at the screen. She glanced over at him with a sad smile on her face. A split second later she dropped to the carpet, rolled, kicked Tohi's legs out from under him, and leaped back into standing position. Before he could even shriek, her boot was on his neck. Just a tiny bit more pressure, and she would crush his windpipe.

"Mr. Tohi, who is captain of this ship?" She released a bit of pressure, to allow him access to his lungs.

"You are, Captain."

"Who is my number one? Who is the person I can count on through thick and thin? Who has my back?"

"I do."

"I don't think you do, Commander. I need to trust my number one. And the only thing I trust you to do is step over my steaming corpse to assume command at the first possible opportunity. Allow me to tell you what you are going to do now. You are going to go to your cabin. You are going to gather your things. Then you are going to head for the escape pods. You're going to get into one of them, and you're going to go back to Sol Station. And you'll do it quickly, because every second you delay will mean a longer trip home for you. Mr. Fin, how long will it take Commander Tohi to return home from our current location at a pod's top speed?"

"Checking, sir," Fin said, his voice shaking. "Four months. Sir."

"If we finish before you get home, we'll give you a lift on our return trip. But for now, I want you off my ship." She turned to Raj. "Weaponer, call a security detail up here to escort Commander Tohi to his cabin, and then to his pod. Oh, and Mr. Raj, until I select a new number one, you'll be acting in that role. Any objections?"

Raj's eyes were full of approval and admiration. "None, sir."

"Good to hear it. I won't tolerate insubordination on this ship. We have a chain of command, and all of our lives depend on it. Attitude gets people killed, Mr. Tohi." She removed her boot from his neck. "I want you to think about that on your long voyage home."

JEFF LOOKED up from his breakfast to see Emma approaching.

"Can't a guy enjoy his eggs?"

"Are you enjoying your eggs?" Emma paused in front of the table and jutted out one hip.

"Not really."

"Then I guess a guy can't. C'mon. We're ready for you."

"I'm gonna finish my fucking eggs," Jeff said. "So have a seat."

Emma smirked, but sat. "The food isn't bad here," she noted.

"Yeah, I got that. Is the cuisine always so good at top-secret joints?"

"I wouldn't know. But my guess is that we just lucked out and got a good cook."

"Who're *we,* by the way?" Jeff asked. He picked up a slice of toast and added some jam to it from a covered jar on the table.

"The *team.* You'll meet them soon enough. How are you doing?"

Jeff chewed and narrowed his eyes. "Define *doing.*"

"How are you feeling?"

"Physically?"

"Sure. We can start there."

"I feel great. Better than I have in years. I'm rested. I'm healthy." He shrugged. "Great."

"And emotionally?"

Jeff put the toast back on his plate and ran the napkin across his lips. "Look, Dr. Stewart, I don't really know you, and I don't feel comfortable—"

"I get it, Captain, but let's be clear about something. This project has a chain of command. When Jennings isn't on site, I'm in charge."

"Why isn't Jennings on site?"

"He has…other things to attend to."

"And Jo…Captain Taylor?"

"Her too."

"What things?"

"Need to know, Captain."

He tossed his toast down and licked the jam off his thumb.

"So let's try this again. Because I'm not your mother, I'm not your girlfriend, I'm not your clergyperson, and I'm not your shrink. I'm your commanding officer. How are you doing emotionally?"

Jeff nodded, pursing his lips but not looking at her. "If that's the case, *sir*, I… Look, Doctor, I'm sure I *have* feelings. I just…don't always know what they are. Okay?"

Emma smiled wryly. "So you're basically saying you're male."

Jeff smirked. He dabbed another piece of toast in the egg yolk rampant on his plate. "I'm…different."

"How so?"

"Before, when I was…before I was…before the Ulim deposited me back in Anchorage, let's put it that way—"

"Okay. Before then?" Emma leaned forward on her elbows.

"Before then I was…I just wanted to be as far away from people as possible."

"Captain Taylor told me something about that."

Jeff nodded. He knew Jo had been hurt—that he had hurt her. His eyes moved back and forth as he remembered.

"Go on."

"I wanted to get as far away as possible—not from her—from…everybody. Because—"

"Because of Catskill?"

"Who told you about Catskill?"

"I was read in. I had to be, Captain. Jennings couldn't possibly have left me in command of you without telling me about it."

He couldn't look at her. He swallowed and gave a barely perceptible nod. "I…a lot of people died there…because of me. I figured if I just wasn't around people, they wouldn't be in any danger, you know?"

"If you'll pardon my saying so, Captain, that's bordering on narcissistic."

"Narcissistic?"

Emma leaned back and tapped her fingers on the table. "The danger has nothing to do with you. We both work for the CDF. People will always be in danger."

"It has to do with me when I'm in charge."

"Being in charge doesn't make you omnipotent. I read the reports, Captain. No one—not a single investigation of the Catskill incident—even hinted at an error in judgment on your part."

"I'm still responsible. But…I feel differently now than… before I went out to New Manila."

"Different how?" She looked up and met his eyes.

"I don't need to slink off under a rock now."

"No? What do you need, then?"

"I need revenge."

"Against who?"

"Who do you think?"

"Is this still a Catskill thing?"

"No, it isn't a fucking Catskill thing. It's a Prox thing." Jeff rubbed his fingers over a beard that was beginning to fill in again. "Look, right or wrong, I blamed myself for Catskill. But even though I was there at New Manila, I know I didn't cause it. *They* did. And I want blood."

"It might not be red."

"It better not be."

Emma's lips turned up in the beginning of a smile. In spite of himself, Jeff found he liked her...a little more than he should have.

She stood and straightened her uniform. "So what are we waiting for?"

Jeff picked up his tray and carried it to the bus station. Then he fell into step beside her. "I wish I knew what we were trying to accomplish here."

"We're exploring. Looking for a possible edge. It's R&D."

"I don't see it."

Emma laughed. "Jo said something about you being a meathead."

"Gee, thanks."

"No offense intended. Look, if this is folly, it's Jennings' folly. He's a visionary. It's why he's an Admiral."

"Jennings is a visionary? Are you on morphex?"

"I've worked under Jennings for more than five years now. He has a sixth sense about things. He trusts his gut...and it's usually right. He sees potential in plans that sound crazy. He spots talent in people others dismiss."

They were nearly at the big, boxy prefabricated building.

It loomed over them long before they arrived, much larger than it looked from a distance. Emma held the door for him. Jeff blinked as his eyes adjusted. It seemed no less voluminous inside than it had outside. Instead of being carved up into floors and rooms, the building housed one large, cavernous space. One half of the mammoth building was taken up with machinery that seemed both antiquated and arcane. The other was filled with cubicles and room dividers —all of which felt to him ineffectual, given the enormity of the unbroken space just above their heads.

Emma led him to the bank of cubicles. Standing near a door was a hard mountain of a soldier, a very large laser rifle slung at his side. His uniform-t was pulled tight over his brown neck, and his bulging arm muscles had obviously been modified, probably on a 'roid regimen begun in grade school. "This is Lieutenant Suarez. He'll be providing security for us here." Jeff nodded at Suarez, but the big man's hard, glassy eyes betrayed no response.

Emma then waved her hand toward a middle-aged man who looked like his people might have come from Korea or Japan. He was sitting stock upright, his eyes rolled up into his head, obviously reading something on his neural. He must have sensed motion, because he lowered his eyes and smiled. "Captain, this is Dr. Tan," Emma introduced them. "He's a medical doctor. He's going to make sure we don't kill you while we do…whatever it is we're doing."

Jeff shook hands with the doctor, but withdrew his hand quickly because the man shook with the conviction of a limp toad. Jeff hated that. It made him want to squeeze the man's hand until a bone snapped, but he resisted that temptation. "Dr. Tan is going to be monitoring your vitals and tending to you should there be anything…should…anything unforeseen happen." Jeff nodded and Emma continued. "And I will be monitoring the gravimeter, looking for any unexpected local phenomenon, but most especially for any warping of spacetime."

Jeff nodded. "Let's squash," he said, rolling up his sleeves. "So what is that?" He indicated the massive arcane machinery with a flick of his chin.

Emma turned toward the half of the room filled with the looming machinery. "*That* is your power source. That's primarily why we're here."

"Looks like something out of a Jules Verne novel."

"It does indeed," Emma conceded. "But it was actually built in the mid-twentieth century by Canadian researchers trying to find a limit to the load of a proposed power grid."

"Did they find it?" Jeff asked.

"At about one-one-hundredth of the capacity of that thing."

"So it was a bit of overkill at the time."

"Yes. Lucky for us."

"Surely we have this thing beat by a mile by now?" Jeff said.

"Yes and no," Emma said. "The fact is that most of our electronics use far less power than even your basic toaster did in the mid-twentieth century. We just have no need to generate power on this scale anymore."

"And our propulsion systems—"

"Have electronics, but aren't driven by electricity."

"Right. Of course."

"So sure, we could have rigged up something new and flashy, but why? As Victorian as it looks to you and me, Captain, it will do the job just fine."

"Okay, I'm convinced," Jeff said. "So what's the plan?"

"This way," Emma turned and began walking at a brisk pace toward the east side of the building. Jeff had to nearly trot to keep up with her, but he found he enjoyed the challenge. And the view. The pear-shape of her bottom moved like a ringing bell as she walked, and Jeff found it impossible not to watch. As he did, he felt his own chemistry changing.

A few moments later, they reached an area a good distance away from the cubicles. In front of them was a horseshoe-shaped structure about nine feet high, made of a dull black material. Jeff reached out and touched it. "Rubber?"

"Close enough," Emma said. "It's a shielded polymer. Nothing gets in, nothing gets out. Not electricity, not radiation, not spiders."

"This is my office, then," Jeff said.

"We hope you like it," Emma smiled briefly. Her short blonde hair bobbed as she jerked her head back to the structure. She keyed in a code and a small door appeared, similar to the kind Jeff was used to seeing on starships between structural sections. In space these could be used as airlocks in case one part of the ship is damaged and depressurizes. "This way."

Jeff followed Emma in. "Will my standard code work on that?"

"Yep," Emma answered ahead of him. The polymer wall seemed to be massive. Jeff estimated it was a solid eight feet. The doorway was, in fact, a short hallway, spilling them into a room that looked like a cross between a hospital room and a starship bridge. Where the captain's chair would be was what looked like an oversized easy chair, ash gray in color, with a matching gray linen headrest. Behind it were IV poles with bags hanging and ready to go. Some kind of medical monitoring device stood to one side. Jeff saw thick rubber cables running into a hole in the floor. A snake's nest of smaller cables lay in a woven basket beside it. "Quaint," Jeff said to no one in particular.

Around the periphery of the room holomonitors were projecting a variety of information. Jeff turned as Dr. Tan entered and watched as he made his way to the chair. He pulled a small metal rolling stool out of some cubbyhole Jeff hadn't noticed and sat down on it, pulling the tangle of cables out of the basket. "We've set you up with a head, right over there, Captain," he said. "Might want to use it before we hook you up."

"I'm fine," Jeff said.

Tan patted the large chair. "Time to get you wired in, then."

Jeff's eyebrows lifted as he caught and held Emma's eyes. She nodded at him encouragingly, and he strode the few paces to the chair and sat down. Tan instantly went to work, first plugging a mercy cord into his neural port, then laying out a series of wires with nodes and suction cups on the ends of them. "Is *everything* from the twentieth century here?" Jeff asked.

"Doctor Tan needs several readings your neural can't give him," Emma explained.

"Doctor Tan is unnecessarily nosy."

Tan harrumphed, but a slight smile escaped him as he pointed to Jeff's shirt. "You need to lose the laundry, Captain. Just your shirt. If you're cold, I can give you a blanket when we're done."

Jeff crunched forward, and removed his CDF jersey with a single motion, tossing it to the floor.

Jeff thought he caught Emma admiring him, and she looked away a little too quickly. He felt pleased about that. Tan applied some kind of gel to the contact sensors from a small tube, and began fixing them to different places on his torso. "I'm going to do a bit of minor surgery now," Tan said. "I need to insert a PICC line so we can run our IV without having to gift you with a new puncture wound every day. It won't be pleasant, but—"

"What's the IV for?"

"To keep your fluids up, keep your electrolytes balanced, supply you with steroids, stimulants, and anxiolytics—"

"I don't need any fucking anxiolytics."

"To be frank, Captain, that's my call, not yours."

"Just do it," Jeff said, closing his eyes in resignation. He was aware that he was less patient with the man simply because the doctor didn't know how to shake his hand properly. He knew there was something wrong with that, but he didn't care enough to do anything about it.

Tan nodded and picked up what looked like a small power tool. He held the narrow end of it just below Jeff's collarbone, and then judged the angle of its descent. Squinting, Tan changed the angle a fraction of a degree, and touched a node on the handle. Jeff heard a puff of air, and then felt a stab in his chest. The pain followed a moment later. "Jesus fucking—"

"Just hold on," Tan said. He fixed a tube connector to the PICC line, and a moment later the pain subsided.

"You could have blocked that with the neural," Jeff said, a note of accusation in his voice.

"Could have," Tan said. "And I was about to suggest it. But you said—"

"Can we just get this done?" Jeff barked.

Tan's face went blank and he continued his work. A minute later he swiveled on his stool and faced Emma. "He's unpleasant, but ready."

Emma walked over, and with a flick of her chin Tan

surrendered his stool. She sat on it and rolled close to Jeff. "Captain, the next few days are going to be pretty taxing."

"I'm a soldier, Doctor. Taxing comes with the territory."

"We're also working somewhat at cross-purposes. That's just...full disclosure." She smiled a little sadly. "Admiral Jennings wants to exploit whatever...gift...you seem to have acquired for whatever military applications we might uncover. But I'm..."

"You want to advance science."

"Yes."

"And you don't want it to be abused."

"Right."

"Well, doctor, we're just going to have to trust each other. But the thing about that is...well, you scientists have always been on the losing side of that contest."

She didn't answer. What could she say? It was true.

"If you think we're going to pass up an effective weapon just because it might be..." he fished for the word.

"Immoral?" she asked.

He narrowed his eyes. "I thought you were a physicist. Now you're an ethicist?"

"History holds all of us accountable for our behavior, Captain. You look me in the eye and tell me that you're proud of everything you've ever done as a soldier."

He looked down. He felt suddenly very small. "I..."

"Let's just trust each other," Emma said.

"Okay," Jeff agreed.

"So, here's what we need to do first. I want to see if I can measure how far away you can sense things, and how far away you can affect them."

"How are you going to do that?"

"You're going to tell me what you see, focusing on

increasingly distant outposts, and we'll verify your observations by the ansible."

"What if no one answers the ansible?"

"Have you ever known someone not to answer an ansible call?"

"Not if they're alive, no."

"Jeff," Emma placed a tentative hand on his chest. "Don't be difficult."

"Did no one warn you that I had a reputation?"

"You don't need to prove it. Let's have fun with this."

"Fun."

"Yeah. Let's give that a whirl."

Jeff nodded. "All right. Let's have some fun with it."

Emma stood and headed for the exit. "We'll communicate by voice—your chair is fitted with a microphone. Also, when your eyes are open and you're not…under, I suppose…you can see me on the monitors. Also, feel free to use your neural to text."

"And power?" Jeff asked.

"Right over there," Emma pointed beyond the walls of the containment unit toward where the mammoth generator loomed. "We've arranged it to ramp up according to load. So go ahead and draw on it…however you do that…and it *should* keep pace with you. The more you draw, the more it will supply. Its capacity isn't infinite, but I seriously doubt you'll max it out."

"I guess we'll see," Jeff said.

"I guess we will. Good luck, Captain." Stewart turned again and, followed by Tan, left him alone in what seemed to him to be a giant rubber donut.

JO NEEDED a cup of Mayan hot chocolate after her confrontation with Tohi. She felt slightly guilty and wondered if perhaps she'd been too hard on him. As the crew rotation neared she knew exactly what her bridge crew would be talking about in the mess. In twenty-four hours there wouldn't be a single crewmember who hadn't heard the tale —probably wildly exaggerated by that time, which only played in her favor. She didn't know if she'd been too hard on Tohi, but she did know one thing—she wouldn't have any more trouble with her chain of command. She'd have to thank Commander Tohi for that some day. Maybe she'd send flowers.

A blinking red light in her neural alerted her to an incoming message, marked urgent. She looked up and accessed it.

—Engineer Ngoku *en route* to sickbay. Electrical shock while repairing food synthesizer unit in aft mess.

Jo frowned. That should have been a minor repair. She stood and straightened her uniform. "I'm going to supervise a repair. You have the bridge, Mr. Raj."

Raj nodded in acknowledgement and stood to take the con. *I'm going to have to get to know him better,* Jo thought as she headed for the lift. He intrigued her. She also had to admit that she found him attractive. Too young for her, but hot nevertheless.

A few minutes later she entered the aft mess and strode toward the cluster of engineers gathered around a partly disassembled food synthesizer unit. "Captain on deck," one of them shouted when he saw her. The others leaped to their feet and stood at attention.

"As you were," Jo said, clasping her hands behind her back. "Any word on Ensign Ngoku?" she asked.

"They said he was going to be fine, sir." The ranking

engineer in this gaggle was only a lieutenant junior grade, and he looked nervous enough to lose his lunch on her shoes if she didn't put him at ease.

"I'm glad to hear it. Thank you for getting him help so quickly."

"Uh...of course, sir." The man was thin and tall, with flaming red hair. He was starting to sweat.

"What happened?"

"A pretty old-fashioned problem, sir. Some wiring wasn't properly shielded when this unit was installed."

"Isn't everything solid state?"

"Yes, sir, but you still have to get power to it. You'll see that the casing is metal—it's a conductor."

"The casing was in contact with the unshielded wiring," Jo reasoned, "and Ensign Ngoku got quite a shock."

"That's what happened, sir."

"Is that the only thing wrong with the unit?"

"Uh...no sir. Its fabrication is...flawed. If you order apple pie, it comes out looking like oatmeal. In fact, everything comes out looking like oatmeal. Still tastes like apple pie, just not that appetizing."

"Is it spiders?"

The lieutenant chuckled, looking at his shoes momentarily. She read the nametape sewed onto his uniform—*Kerr*. "Oh, no sir. No spiders on this ship."

Jo harrumphed. "How long do you think *that* will last, Mr. Kerr?"

"I...uh...oh, probably about three months, sir."

"Tell me the truth. There are spiders aboard now."

"Uh...yes sir. But not many."

"Right. So it's not spiders. Does the fabrication error have anything to do with the wiring problem?"

"No sir. Ensign Ngoku was investigating the fabrication

errors when he touched the casing, and…well, *zap*." The lieu-tenant looked profoundly uncomfortable.

"How much of a charge did he get?"

"Uh…about 240 volts. But the amps were low, thank God."

"Lieutenant, I'm going to eat my dinner from this machine tonight. I don't expect my steak to look like oatmeal."

"No sir."

She turned on her heel and headed back to the bridge, but the idea of the boredom of sitting in that bridge chair—as shiny as it was—depressed her. She made a course correction and headed for stellar cartography. She'd see how the simula-tions were coming along. And then she'd swing by sickbay. She'd find out for herself how Ensign Ngoku was faring.

———

JEFF WAS surprised at how comfortable the chair was. *It's like floating*, he thought, as he rested back into it. He stared up through the hole in the big rubber donut at the girders of the pre-fab building, painted a pastel aqua by city workers six generations ago. As he thought about them, the plasticity of time collided with the plasticity of space in his imagination, leaving him with a momentary feeling of vertigo. He wondered if repeated squashing changed more than simply his perceptions. What if, every time he entered *that* space, he was a little less in *this* one? The thought terrified him and he put it out of mind immediately.

He heard Dr. Stewart's voice in his ear. "Okay, Captain, we are ready when you are."

"Roger that," he said, enjoying the archaism. He imagined Dr. Stewart turning to Tan and mouthing, "Who's Roger?"

He smiled involuntarily at the thought and closed his eyes. He reached out intuitively, imagining and perceiving the space around him. In his mind's eye, he saw a great light. Turning toward it, it filled the whole of his field of vision. It was the generator—huge and bright and lovely. He imagined himself drifting toward it instinctively. The closer he got, the more power he sensed. He reached out with his hands and took hold of the power. He felt it enter him, filling him, charging him. *This feels fantastic,* he thought. *I'm unlimited! I'm invincible!*

Whoa, cowboy, he reminded himself. *Feeling and being are not the same thing.* He dimly remembered a similar feeling of invincibility when he was a young cadet. That had lasted until the first of their platoon had gotten their heads blown off by a rebel particle cannon. With effort, he turned his mind from the ecstasy of the moment to his purpose. He experimented with the power, drawing now more, now less. He found it was unpredictable until he imagined a rheostat in front of him. In his mind's eye, he reached out and turned it up. The power swelled within him. He turned it back down and felt the power wane. His brain crackled with electricity. The feeling was intoxicating, even at the lower power levels.

"What are you doing, Captain?" Emma's voice asked.

"Just figuring out how to draw power. I think I've got a handle on it now."

"Good. I want you to reach out with your awareness. Power down and go to the periphery and tell me what you see."

Jeff imagined turning down the rheostat, then reached outward with his mind. He saw every creature for a radius that must have extended hundreds of miles. He heard their thoughts, felt their feelings, faced their dilemmas, experienced their joy, their grief, their orgasms. He read a sign. "Route 135, Fermor," he said.

"That's a transport designation—a highway in Winnipeg. Checking…that's a little over 1000 kilometers, due east. Good. What happens if you go north?"

Jeff saw himself turning and reaching out again, sensing far less activity. Mostly the heavier awareness of animals, even plant life. "Snow! I didn't know there even *was* any snow anymore."

"Some, apparently. Good. West?"

He turned again and saw water as far as the eye could see. He felt the slick, heavy awareness of fish, the quick consciousness of the occasional whale. The strangeness of underwater life surprised him and even shook him. "Yeah. Okay. Fish. Wet. Weird."

"Go south."

He turned again, to complete the points of the compass, and felt repelled by the scorching heat of the Idaho desert. There was life there, but not much of it. His mind filled with the quick, instinctual motion of lizards and buzzards and insects. "Okay, communing with the reptiles. Nice. Next?"

"Draw a little power and see how far you can sense."

Jeff turned and imagined the Great Light of the generator. He saw the power entering him, felt it crackle in his finger-tips, as he turned up the rheostat. Then he reached out with his mind again. He felt the circle of his awareness expand. He felt the feelings of a world full of beings—fear and flight, compassion and caring, violence and love—all of it at once, undifferentiated, cacophonous. He discovered he could pick out individuals, could distance himself from the other voices, could even "enter" into the bodies of random people or animals.

He imagined himself "landing." He looked around, and

saw multicolored flags hanging from twine, strung from one building to the next, from posts to trees to the ground. He saw multi-storied stupas side-by-side with office buildings. *I must be as far as I can go without circling back around. This is Tibet, or Nepal...*then he saw a sign. Ladakh. *Okay, then, India,* he thought. *Yep, that's as far as you can go.*

Because of the heat, there wasn't much left of India. Its few thriving places were in high altitudes like this, where the air was still cool enough to support life. The street was bustling, crowded. Jeff felt assaulted by the color, the multitude, the smells. *The smells.* He followed one particular aroma. It caused his stomach to rumble. He hadn't been aware that he was hungry. Breakfast seemed like mere moments ago, but his perception of time was off—he knew that. He followed the smell to a street vendor, grilling chunks of yak meat on short sticks over a small brazier on a handcart.

He floated toward the vendor, savoring the delicious aroma. He reached out, saw himself grabbing at one of the meat sticks, but his fingers passed through them.

"Captain Bowers, what do you see?" Emma's voice was distant, as if heard in a different room.

Jeff was fixated on the meat skewers and didn't answer. He *had* to have one. He gripped India between the fingers of one hand, and Alberta in the fingers of the other, and he drew them together. He held them side by side until he experienced himself being in both places at once. He reached for a skewer again, grabbed it, and watched as the vendor scrambled back in surprise. He put the skewer to his lips and bit off a huge, steaming chunk of yak flesh. The meat was juicy, filling his mouth with savory goodness. He grinned with pleasure as he felt its grease run down his chin. He also noticed that he was still seated on the couch from the lab, now blocking traffic on the narrow, crowded Ladakhi street.

"WHY ISN'T HE SAYING ANYTHING?" Emma groused. She activated her microphone. "Captain, tell us what you're seeing."

"Uh…" Tan said.

"Uh, what?"

"Uh…you've got to look at this."

Emma scowled at the medical doctor, but rushed over to his side and looked at his viewscreens. "What am I supposed be looking at?"

"You're supposed to be looking at life signs," Tan said. "But there aren't any."

"How could there…oh, Jesus." Emma looked up at the larger viewscreens, expecting to see Bowers, blissed out in his chair—or dead. Instead she saw an empty room. She bolted for the isolation ring, Tan and Suarez on her heels. She opened the outer portal hatch and raced inside. Once through the inner portal, she stopped and gasped. The chair was gone. All the cables running to it seemed to have been neatly and uniformly severed. "What the…?" She moved into the room, her jaw dropping, her head swimming. She felt as though she were viewing the whole scene from afar, somehow. She turned and faced Tan and Suarez. "Where the fuck did he go?"

No one said anything. Emma began to chew on her fingernails. She felt her pulse quicken. She was starting to panic. Just then she saw a red light in her neural. She accessed it.

—I think I goofed.

It was from Jeff. She let out a breath and pointed at her eye. "Bowers."

—Where are you?

—Ladakh, apparently. India.

—What the fuck are you doing in Ladakh?

—Eating yak skewers.

—Yak skewers?

—Yes. They're delicious.

Emma blinked. "He's in India. Eating yak skewers," she said to Tan and Suarez.

—I need a ride.

Emma began to laugh.

"What?" asked Tan.

"Mr. Suarez, I hate to do this to you, but we need to get you to Regina. You're on the next military transport to Asia. We have a captain and a chair to retrieve."

Suarez didn't look very happy about this news. She didn't blame him.

—Suarez is on his way.

—Can't you send someone less threatening?

—Man up, Captain.

Emma leaned against the wall of the donut and crossed her arms. "So we know two things. One, Bowers can indeed move something larger than a picture frame."

"That's good, right?" Tan asked.

"That's very good."

"What's the other thing?"

"We know that in about twelve hours he's going to be as sick as a dog. Doctor, we're going to need a prescription for some altitude sickness meds. And Suarez, get going before the captain passes out on the street."

CHAPTER FIVE

"Deseret Colony within hailing range, Captain," Lieutenant Frey said.

"Thank you, Lieutenant. Open a channel," Jo said. She'd been pacing, but she paused and put her hand on the back of her command chair.

"Yes, sir." Frey paused. Then she nodded. "Channel open and acknowledged."

"Deseret Colony, this is the CDF warship *Essex*, estimating our time of arrival in…" she waved at Fin.

"Ninety minutes, Captain," Fin called over his shoulder.

"Ninety minutes. Request permission to approach?"

"Captain, I have visual," Frey announced.

"On screen," Jo said.

There was a ripple and the sea of stars was replaced by the figure of a middle-aged man in uniform. His hair was beginning to thin, but he made up for it with an impressive beard—although his upper lip was clean-shaven. At first Jo thought it was an odd effect, until she remembered a picture of Abraham Lincoln, who also wore his facial hair in the same curious style.

Men and their hair, she thought.

"This is Captain Joleen Taylor of the CDF warship *Essex*. With whom am I speaking?"

"This is General T.I. Warwick of the Deseret Defense Corps."

Jo wondered if his friends called him "T.I." She also noted that he pronounced his name, "WAR-rick," after the English style.

"General, I bring you greetings from the mother planet and the Colonial Defense Fleet."

"I haven't got time for pleasantries, Captain. In case you didn't know, we're going to be under attack in less than twelve hours."

"I am well aware, General, and that's why we're here. We're the advance guard of a whole fleet of CDF forces. We're just a tiny bit faster than they are."

"We're grateful, Captain, but you won't be needed. We told Admiral Jennings not to send ships. We will have the invaders well in hand." Warwick looked distracted, glancing down as if reading something off of a datapad.

Fin glanced up at the captain, his eyebrows riding high on his head in surprise.

"General, I'm heartened by your confidence. But surely a show of overwhelming strength can't be a bad thing in this case. It may act as a deterrent should the Prox get ideas about attacking other Union colonies."

"We've got overwhelming force already. Maybe you're not familiar with—"

"I assure you, General, I have been fully briefed on your capabilities. I'm concerned that you might be underestimating the enemy."

"Turn around, Captain." Warwick looked back up at the camera now. "We've got this."

"General, the fact that we are here is evidence of your tax dollars at work. You've already paid for our support, now—" The viewscreen went blank.

"I believe he just cut us off in mid-transmission, sir," Frey announced.

"The son-of-a-bitch," Jo said. "Weaponer Raj, what can I blow up around here that won't endanger any Mormons?"

"We've got a dead satellite in geosynchronous orbit around Deseret in our direct line of fire, Captain. No electronic activity at all."

"Perfect. Weaponer, load one of our thermonuclear devices—just a small one ought to do. Fire when ready."

Jo watched Raj's hands fly over his controls. Then he glanced up at the viewscreen in order to see the fruit of his labor. The screen dimmed as the exterior cameras were overwhelmed by the light of the explosion. There was no sound, of course. Once the cameras adjusted, they only saw the emptiness of space where a large rock had been moments before.

"They're hailing us, sir," Frey said, the corner of her mouth turned up in a wry smile.

"On screen." Jo took her seat.

"What in the name of the Prophet's Nanny are you trying to do?" General Warwick spluttered, his eyes wide with alarm.

"Apparently you have a short attention span," Jo said. "I have found that sometimes you have to wave a shiny object in front of people with short attention spans."

"That was a white salamander move, Captain, and it will go in my report."

"Excellent. I'm here to make sure you live long enough to file one."

Warwick looked angry enough to erupt. Jo could see that

he was physically shaking. "Put us where we'll do the most good, General. I'm sending over a manifest of the other ships underway, along with their firepower and approximate time of arrival." She nodded at Frey, who began to cull the information into a transmittable datapacket.

Jo was reminded of someone else who had trouble accepting help. She rose and took a couple steps forward toward the viewscreen, trying to create an illusion of intimacy. "Look, General, this is your fight. But we're your friends. It's no shame on you if you let us help. We *want* to help. We value Deseret's role in the Colonial Union. Let your friends be your friends. This is what friends *do* for each other."

Warwick grumbled something inaudible.

"Do you want me to amplify and replay that, Captain?" Frey asked.

Jo held her hand up, fending off Frey's question for the moment.

"I'm sorry, General, I didn't catch that."

"I want you with the reserves. I'll call you out only if we need you. As for the other ships on the way—what a colossal waste of resources. We'll have these filthy invaders mopped up before they even get here."

"I hope you're right, General. But if you're not…we've got your back."

<hr />

JENNINGS SAW the blue light in his neural and checked the message. It was from Liu.

—Dr. Stewart is waiting for you.

—Send her in.

A moment later, the door slid open and Emma Stewart

walked in. She strode to his desk and presented herself, hands clasped behind her back.

"Doctor."

"Admiral."

"I hear you have good news. I could use some good news."

"Yes…we've made some real progress."

"Sit down, Doctor," Jennings waved her over to a compact black leather chair. "Whiskey?"

"No, I…why the hell not?" she smiled. "I haven't really let myself celebrate, after all. Too much to do."

"High time, then." Jennings poured two fingers each into crystal glasses and set one of them on his desk in front of the doctor. He sat back in his own seat. "Yes. I've read the report. Hell of a thing. I laughed out loud when I read about India."

"We might have seen that as a setback, but it was actually a breakthrough. And it was his first time out—since we've been monitoring him, that is. In the couple weeks since we've started working together, he's fine-tuned his ability. If we were talking about a merely physical phenomenon, I'd say he has vastly improved his fine motor control."

"Don't want to say he's improved his fine mind control? Same acronym."

"I'd rather avoid it," she smirked. "Since I finished that report, we've made even more progress."

"Do tell."

"Captain Bowers is now able to locate or place objects at precise GPS coordinates."

"How is he gauging those?"

"Neural."

"Ah. I should have guessed that." Jennings took a sip from his glass and made a pleased face.

"And he has succeeded in moving both a Humvee, and then a house."

"Was anyone *in* the house?"

"No, thank God."

"So how did that go?"

"Let's just say there's a cornfield in Saskatchewan that is *very* flat right now."

"Is the house still flattening unsuspecting farms in Saskatchewan?"

"No, he moved it back."

"Um…didn't that—"

"Sever all the power lines? Yes. We're repairing them now."

Jennings shook his head and laughed.

"Is he behaving himself?"

"Captain Bowers? He and Tan don't really get along, but ever since the India trip he and Suarez have been hanging out."

"And how are *you*?"

"Fine."

"Fine? What the hell does that mean, Doctor?"

Emma looked away but didn't answer. "I think we're ready. If what you want to do with this is move troops or warships instantaneously…we're going to need to move our lab to space. And we're going to need a ship."

"A ship?"

"If you want to move a warship, we have to practice on a ship—some ship, any ship. Preferably something small, at least at first. Then we'll take what we've learned and ramp it up. It's no different from what we've been doing. This is just…it's the next logical step."

"Why can't we just have him move a warship now?"

"Because it's imprudent and unethical and could be potentially disastrous. If you want the brass—"

"I *am* the brass, in case you haven't noticed."

"If you want your *fellow* brass to embrace this project, we don't want any…setbacks."

"You're right. Of course. I just…" Jennings looked at his viewscreen, set to peer into deep space.

"What's happening out there? At Deseret? With Captain Taylor?"

"I wish I knew. The ansible is quiet, which I'm taking as a good sign. I just wish—"

"You wish you could help them *now*."

"Yes."

"We're getting there, Admiral. Think of this as the last time any of our colonies or allies will face anything alone."

———

—WEAPONER RAJ, please meet me in my consult station.

A moment later, the door whooshed open and the Weaponer saluted.

"Have a seat, number one," Jo said. The consult station was a small office just off the bridge for the captain's private use. She expected Raj to be quick, but his appearance was eerily instantaneous, as if he had been poised by the door, waiting for her call. And what if he had been? Wasn't a senior officer's ability to anticipate the needs of his commanding officer an asset?

Raj sat opposite her, looking uncomfortable. Jo set a cup of Mayan hot chocolate in front of him. He looked at it as if it were a snail.

"Report," she ordered.

Raj's eyebrows rose slightly, but then he started in. "We completed the scenario drills at fourteen hundred hours, sir."

"Did we get that response time up?"

"We did, and we exceeded our goals by twenty-one seconds."

"That's excellent, number one. Truly excellent."

"I must say, Captain, at first I thought that the drilling schedule was excessive, but I can see two benefits. Not only have we exceeded our best response time, but the crew is relaxed rather than nervous."

"Too busy to worry," Jo nodded. She took a sip of her own cocoa.

"It was a shrewd idea."

"Flattery is not a good strategy, Raj."

He smiled. "It was honest, sir. No flattery here."

Weaponer Raj had surprised her. She admired his easy confidence. She also couldn't stop thinking about him. She hated these shipboard crushes. She was far too susceptible to them, and all she could do was wait them out. This one would pass. They always did.

"I've been studying the Deseret defenses," Raj said.

"And?"

"And they've got six times the firepower at their disposal as New Manila had."

"Will it be enough?"

"That is the question, sir."

"Do you have a guess?"

"Based on what I have seen from the New Manila transmissions, I think they're going to get their assess handed to them."

Jo nodded. She'd come to the same conclusion. "You can't tell them that."

"No sir."

"They don't want to hear anything from us."

"No."

Jo dropped her eyes and stared at the gentle rippling on the surface of her cocoa. The silence was long, and Jo was amazed at Raj's comfort with it. He surprised her at every turn. And pleased her.

"I...this might be silly, but Chief Engineer Laru and I have been working on a...a secret project," Jo said.

Raj cocked his head. He still hadn't touched his cocoa.

"What kind of project?" he asked.

"A...a defensive weapon, I suppose."

He scowled, no doubt wondering why, as Weaponer, he was only finding out about this now. Jo held her palm up to ward off his protest, however unspoken. "I know, I know, but I thought it was kind of a silly idea in the first place, and I didn't know if it would even work, in the second."

"I'm listening, Captain."

She heard the note of disappointment in his voice. Disappointment in *her*. It hurt.

"Number one, have you ever heard of an electric fence?"

"Certainly. We had them in Nepal, to deter the goat rustlers."

"Do you mean to tell me that in your own lifetime, you dealt with goat rustlers?"

He shrugged. "You have goats—someone is going to want to rustle them."

She smiled and shook her head slowly. "Okay, so you run a current through the wire. And if someone touches the wire—"

"They get an electric shock."

"And does it have to be wire?"

"It has to be metal, or some kind of conductor."

"What is the hull of our ship made of, Number One?"

"Iconel."

"Is it a conductor?"

"Yes, it's a very good..." he trailed off, his eyes darting back and forth as he grasped her thought.

"We aren't really in any danger until the Prox land on the surface of our ships."

Raj nodded, his face brightening. "We need an electric fence."

"That's just what I was thinking."

Raj's face darkened. "The Envoy fired an EMP burst through the hull—it didn't work."

"EMP is not raw voltage. Anything that lights on our hull is going to be met with 50,000 volts."

"Volts don't really matter. What will the amperage be?"

"Five hundred."

"Will that be enough to knock a Prox on its ass?"

"I think we're about to find out."

AN ALERT LIT up in Jeff's neural.

—Meet me at the starboard docks. I want to show you something.

It was from Emma. Jeff nodded and stood up. *Good. I'm going stir crazy anyway.*

He quickly navigated Sol Station and arrived at the docks in less than five minutes. It was always a busy, bustling area, and he scanned the hurrying crowd. *Maybe I just beat her here?* he wondered. Then he saw her. She broke into a grin and waved, jogging over to him. As she ran he felt a strange, familiar and mostly unwelcome emotion rise from the dead. *I could love this woman,* he thought. *And I shouldn't.*

"Captain," she said, slightly winded. She touched his elbow.

"Doctor," he answered. "What's up?"

"It's here." She tugged at his sleeve and started walking toward the bay windows.

The sleeve-tugging felt a little too playful. *Is she flirting with me?* he wondered. *Or is that just wishful thinking?* He followed her to the window.

It was really a large viewing port out into space, as high as two decks, and twice as wide. The field of stars was brilliant, frenzied, completely unlike the filtered light he experienced when on earth. He thrilled at the sight of it. Large ships in varying stages of approach or departure glided around the docks. Sol Station was the busiest spaceport in the colonies, and that was never so evident as at its docks.

"What am I looking at?" he asked.

"That," Emma pointed.

He followed the direction of her finger. "The *Sahib*?"

"No, to the left of her. The *Bohr*."

It was a small vessel, decked out in the blue and tan of the Colonial Science Corps. It looked to him that a full crew complement might be around ten crewmen. There were no weapons to speak of. The engines were standard propulsion. It was also old—perhaps fifty years old or more, gauging from the design.

"Uh…nice dinosaur."

"True. But it's *our* dinosaur."

"What do you mean?"

"Jennings just assigned her to our project."

"She needs to be assigned to a metals reclamation unit."

"Stop," she slapped his shoulder. "It's a starter ship."

He nodded. "If I can move *that*…"

"*When* you can move that—safely and accurately—we'll move on to bigger things."

"Why not just start with something useful—like a light battlecruiser?"

"Captain, I know you're impatient. And that might make you a good military commander, but it would make you a lousy scientist. For us it's all about baby steps."

He raised his eyebrows and faced her. "Baby steps."

"Yep. One test at a time. Change one thing, then test again."

"You people drive me nuts. Just fill it with marines and let's fucking head for Deseret."

"Are you always so eager for battle?" She smiled sadly.

The question caught him off guard. He looked away, back to the field of stars. "I'm *never* eager for battle. No sane person who's ever seen it is."

"Then what's your rush?"

"I've seen enough people die in my time, and if I'm in a position to stop it…"

"Then you should."

"Then I should."

She nodded. "I can respect that. But look at it from my perspective. You want to get there with troops and firepower—"

"Damn straight."

"I want to get you there in one piece so you can do some good. Can you respect *that*?"

He looked her in the eye. He saw her sincerity. He nodded.

"Good," she said, turning back to the port window. "And to that end, we're going to spend the next week refurbishing the old girl."

"Are you going to update that engine?"

"Why do we need to?"

"It'll only do…" he trailed off. "Oh. *I'm* the engine."

"Bingo," she said, smiling.

She must think I'm a bigger meathead than Jo does, he thought.

"But we *are* going to rip her guts out and put in a new control matrix. And I'm going to personally supervise outfitting her with a sensor web so we can measure whatever unholy thing you're doing to spacetime."

"Anything I can do?"

"Nothing I can think of. We want you to rest."

"I hate fucking resting."

"You can't do it all yourself, Captain."

"You sound like my father."

"At least I don't sound like your mother. I dated a guy once who…never mind. Look, we want you to rest. The squashing will take it out of you, especially something that big—"

"I'm getting better at that," Jeff insisted.

Emma moved her head back and forth in an equivocating gesture. "Just the same, we want you at 110%."

"Fuck that."

"Captain!" She feigned offense.

"I'm just…"

"Bored?"

He didn't answer. "What's first up?"

"Fumigation, what else? We can't do a damn thing until we clear out all the spider nests."

Captain Taylor gripped the back of her chair as she watched the first of the Prox warships drop out of superluminal space. She was too nervous to sit and tried not to bite her nails—unsuccessfully. She turned to Frey. "Zoom in to wherever the most action is, please, Lieutenant. You're going to have the most work to do."

They were already at priority alert status. She had jiggered the schedules to put her best people in their seats at this moment. The second stringers could grouse—and they probably would—but such is the prerogative and the duty of command. She'd try to make it up to them somehow—if they survived.

The main viewscreen magnified the Prox ship. Scanners recognized it as what was left of the *Envoy,* which had been lost at New Manila. Jo wondered if all of their ships were captured. Two more dropped into normal space behind them, taking flanking positions. Just ahead of them, Jo could see the arrayed forces of the Deseret Defense Corps encircling their planet, their promised land, their Zion. She had no doubt that the Mormons would put up one hell of a fight. They had a reputation in the CDF for being comfortable with authority structures, clean-cut as unholy fuck, and merciless in battle. She expected no less of these Mormons.

They took a defensive tack, which surprised her. None of the DDC ships moved as the Prox dropped out of superlux, but maintained their formation around Deseret. She had expected a more aggressive tactic, but who knew what Warwick had up his sleeve?

She realized she had chewed her thumbnail down to its quick only when it started hurting like hell. She wiped her thumb on her uniform and kept her eyes riveted on the screen. "Weaponer, I want every one of our torpedo tubes full, and every backup in the queue."

"Already done, Captain. We are ready to deploy our full arsenal at your command."

She had expected no less. Raj was one hell of a guy. She was thinking of making him her permanent number one, then realized she didn't have a permanent command. *Ah well,* she thought. *A girl can dream.*

"Prox soldiers detaching, sir," Frey said, and moved to zoom in on the advance alien warship. They were almost invisible, the soldiers. Jo tried to distinguish the different species, but they were too far away to make out. They were just dots, really.

"They don't have any fighters?" Fin asked.

"Oh, they have fighters, Lieutenant, but they're not ships. They're just…aliens. Didn't you read your briefing?" She glanced away from the screen long enough to scowl at her navigator.

"Uh…of course. But reading it in the abstract and seeing it in front of you…"

"They're two different things," she finished his sentence. "I get it. Number one, how long before the first of the CDF support ships arrives?"

"Twelve hours, sir."

She knew that. She just hoped that somehow, when it actually came down to it, it would be different. Better. It wasn't.

"Deseret forces at maximum shields. Long-range sniper cannons on both moons at full power and trained on the enemy, sir."

"We can do a bit of that, can't we?"

"I suggest we send two 30-megaton torpedoes on an elliptical course toward their support ships and take them out now."

"I think that's a splendid call, but unfortunately it's not ours to make. Deseret has nuclear torpedoes, too, and no doubt they've got a strategy. I'm not about to interfere with that. We'll withhold our own assault until ordered to."

Raj scowled at his panel and didn't look at her. "Yes, Captain."

"First of the Prox warriors approaching DDC ships, sir. Contact in fifteen seconds."

Every ship in the fleet with a shot at the alien soldiers had opened fire. She thrilled to see that some of the little black dots disintegrated and disappeared. Jo leaned over the back of her chair, trying to get closer to the screen. "Zoom in, Mr. Frey."

"Okay, but it'll be grainy," she said.

"That's fine. I want to see what we're up against with my own eyes." She'd seen the vids from New Manila, but there was something about seeing it as it was happening that felt qualitatively different to her.

The screen resolved, and she was relieved to see that the image of the defending ship wasn't as distorted as she'd feared.

"Sir, shouldn't we be wary of being hit where we're *not* looking?"

"Stealth does not seem to be in their playbook, number one. And they don't need it."

She held her breath as the first of the Prox soldiers alighted on one of the Deseret ships. A nearby ship fired at the approaching soldier, but, wary of hitting its own side, its shots went wide as the soldier approached. All around the ship, other soldiers landed; some they could see, but others were out of sight. The Prox seemed to take a moment to orient themselves. "What are they waiting for?" Jo asked.

"Perhaps they are fixing a firm grip on the hull," Laru suggested. Jo nodded. It was plausible.

Just then one of the stick-like legs struck downward.

"They're like crabs…" Fin breathed.

"No crab was ever this deadly, Lieutenant," Jo said. Then her jaw dropped as she watched the soldier rip a sheet of metal plating from the hull.

"Holy Christ," Fin breathed.

While its dactyl pulled the metal away from the hull, its pereopods began to scramble inside the hole it had made, ripping out wire and insulation. Jo watched as detritus floated free from the breach. Then there was an explosion as a seal was broken and air rushed into the vacuum of space, carrying with it everything not fastened down, including some Mormon militiamen who jerked and gasped before succumbing to the vacuum of space.

"That's horrible," Frey said, turning her face away from the viewscreen.

"Okay, message received," Jo said. "I want every member of this crew belted in, now." She circled around her command chair and finally sat in it, fastening the restraints. It was obvious that the chair had been built for a bigger body than hers, but she was confident it would hold her. Raj triggered an alert that began sounding all over the ship with a message no one could miss and no one would ignore—belt in.

Jo estimated that over a hundred Prox soldiers had landed on that one ship alone, and all of them were busy ripping up iconel sheeting. It was then that she saw the first of the worker Prox circling around to collect the sheets of hull plating, although some soldiers were pausing to simply eat them. The Prox ignored the shots fired by nearby vessels, none of which came close enough to do any damage. Every now and then a Prox soldier or worker would explode en route to the ship, but there were always more behind. The sheer number of them was staggering, well beyond Jo's ability to estimate.

Fortunately, she didn't need to. "Weaponer Raj, how many of the enemy have been deployed?"

Raj didn't even need to look down. "Six hundred fifty thousand, sir. And counting."

"Pull back, Mr. Frey. I want to see what's happening elsewhere."

The screen zoomed out, and Jo's eyes widened in horror as she saw every visible ship in the Deseret Defense Corps being actively dismantled. Every ship was firing like mad at the approaching Prox, and although they hit a good number of targets, their efforts did not even begin to stop the flood of enemy soldiers.

"This is a slaughter," Fin said.

"It's not a surprise," Jo said. She forced herself to turn away from the screen. "Mr. Frey, contact General Warwick and ask permission to enter the fight."

"Yes sir."

Just then there was a blaze of light as nuclear torpedoes hit their targets. Jo was glad she had not been looking directly at the screen, and she shielded her eyes until the screen adjusted. "What did they hit them with?"

"50-megatons, in a coordinated strike of fifteen torpedoes."

Jo gripped the armrest of her command chair until her fingers were white. "And? And?" she asked, despite her efforts to be a calm presence. It seemed like it took an eternity for the fireball to subside and the screen to adjust. When it did, Jo saw that a corner of a massive triangular ship had been blown off. "Score one for our team," she breathed. But it was clear it would not be enough. The ships capable of firing that kind of power were being dismantled before their very eyes.

"Mr. Frey, open a channel to General Warwick," Jo said.

"I…channel is open, sir, but no one is responding."

"General Warwick, this is Captain Taylor of the CDF *Essex*. Request permission to join the fray."

Jo heard nothing back. "Repeat my request, Mr. Frey."

"Repeating, sir."

Jo watched as worker Prox removed steel plates by the score, by the hundreds, in a fire-brigade operation from their prey back to their ship. There was a flash from one of the Mormon ships and Jo bit the stub of her nail again as she watched equipment, furniture, and crew members float into space as its lost air pressure forced everything into the vacuum.

"Shit," Fin said. He turned and looked at the captain. So did Laru. So did Raj.

"Okay, fuck it," Jo said, pounding the arm of her command chair. "The chain of command here has obviously broken down. Fin, set a course for fly-by stingray attacks on the three Prox carrier vessels. I want us in and out of there in seconds. Weaponer Raj, coordinate with Mr. Fin so that we launch our nukes at our closest proximity to the enemy. Start with the damaged ship, aim straight into the worst of the damage. Hopefully the shields will be damaged in that section, too. Let's go kick a bastard while he's down."

CHAPTER SIX

J eff poured himself a scotch. He had been drinking a lot of scotch lately. He poured it back into the bottle, spilling a little as he did so. *That was a waste,* he thought. *Should have just drunk it.* He wasn't drinking to relax. He certainly wasn't drinking socially—he was alone in the tiny cabin assigned to him on Sol Station.

"I'm drinking because I'm bored," he said aloud. "Well, so long as you know that." He poured himself another glass. This time, he sipped at it. He sat on the single chair in his cabin and put his feet up on his bunk. He swilled the scotch on his tongue, savoring its acrid smokiness. A song from his childhood kept going through his head. He hated that song. He took another sip and forced himself to think about something else.

But there were too many things he *shouldn't* think about. He had walled off a whole section of his brain relating to Catskill, and he was smart enough not to venture there, even when he was drunk. But there were parallels to the New Manila episode that haunted him. Like Catskill, New Manila had been a slaughter. Like Catskill he had watched it happen

—at least, he had watched the enemy feasting on its victory. Like Catskill, he was the only one who walked away.

He knew it wasn't the same. He wasn't in command on New Manila. He wasn't responsible for the people who died there. New Manila was not his fault. But the similarities pricked at him, opened old wounds, made him want another drink. And since there was no place he needed to be, no one to whom he needed to report, nothing he needed to do…

Jeff opened one bleary eye. He saw the bottle, the bottle he had just opened, saw that it was half empty. He knew that after that much alcohol, he ought to be sick as a dog for a couple days. But his new body handled alcohol like a twenty-year-old. He felt a pocket of sick in his stomach and his head ached a little. He felt slightly fluish, sweaty. But otherwise… fine. He opened the other eye, and jumped, startled.

"Oh shit," he yelled percussively.

"Hello, Jeff."

Danny was sitting on his bed. Jeff sat up, fully awake and alert now. "Water…I need some water." He rose and grabbed a coffee cup and went into the hall. He watched the door slide closed behind him, then turned, passed the communal bathroom, into the break room. It wasn't a mess exactly, just a small kitchen area shared by everyone in his cluster of cabins. He filled the cup with cool water from the dispenser and drank it down. He filled it again and drank that, too. He filled it a third time and then walked back to his cabin.

He paused at the door. Had he really seen Danny on his bed? Or was that the whiskey talking? He pressed the OPEN button. The door slid open and he looked at the bed. Danny was there, smiling patiently. He let the door close again and rested his head on it when it had stopped moving. "Shit shit shit shit shit."

It can't really be Danny, he thought. *It must...*he jerked upright. *It must be the Ulim.*

He punched the button again, and again the door slid open. Jeff stepped inside. "Hello, Danny."

"Hello, Jeff. It is good to see you looking so well."

What's he talking about? I look like hell, Jeff thought. "You are the Ulim."

Danny smiled. "We are the Ulim."

Jeff nodded. "I need to...I...thank you."

Danny cocked his head.

"For saving my life. For sending me home."

"You are welcome."

"But I'm guessing you didn't come here so I could be grateful at you."

"No. We are here because you surprise us."

"I? Surprise you? How?'

"Our..." he seemed to fish for a word, then found it. "Methods. For travel. We thought they were...beyond you. It never occurred to us that just by witnessing our...method... you would be able to do it yourself. Especially since you only saw it happen once."

Jeff nodded and resumed his seat, facing Danny. "I don't think I could explain it to you. I mean, Dr. Stewart has been trying to get me to explain it to her ever since I got back, and I can't. I just can't, because I don't understand it myself. But I remember how it felt..." Jeff paused to consider how ironic that was. He had spent so much of his adult life trying not to feel, and yet it was his capacity for feeling that allowed him to do this. "You know when I remember it best? When I dream."

Danny smiled at this. "That makes a lot of sense to us. Our life is a shared dream, in a way. So much of what we do is shaped by this...dreaming." His smile faded. "But the fact that you have learned to do it is…unfortunate. You are not ready for it."

Jeff scowled. "What do you mean by 'you'? Do you mean me, Jeff Bowers? Or do you mean humanity?"

"We are saying both."

Jeff allowed a little heat into his voice. "Who are you to say I'm not ready for it? Or that humankind isn't ready for it?"

"We are the ones who know about this…method. We are the ones who understand it, who understand what is at stake and what is at risk."

"What are you talking about?" Jeff asked. His head hurt. This was not a conversation he wanted to be having when his head hurt.

"The universe is far more fragile than you suppose it to be. It persists only because of a perfectly balanced set of forces. You are manipulating these forces. It is like…forgive us for saying this, but you are like a child playing with a bomb you found in an abandoned lot."

Jeff wondered where the Ulim had gleaned that analogy. Probably from his own mind. When he was a cadet, he remembered a child who had found a mine in an abandoned lot and had blown himself up trying to take it apart. He'd felt sick about it at the time. If the Ulim needed a disturbing or affecting memory, it would be hard to find a better one. He nodded. He got what they were saying. But… "I think you're overreacting."

Danny cocked his head again. "Are we?"

"Sure. Look, we're being careful. We're starting small. We're scaling up slowly, one thing at a time. You didn't learn this method overnight—you developed it—"

"Over several thousand years, yes."

That stopped Jeff cold. He had only known how to squash for a few weeks. Still… "We're being careful."

Danny looked down, his smile fading. He shook his head. "It does not work that way. Careful is not enough. Small… that is irrelevant. Size is irrelevant. Scale is irrelevant. And scale is everything."

"Now you're sounding like the Ulim again."

Danny allowed himself a smile at that. "We are always the Ulim." He looked Jeff in the eye. "Even the smallest jump, if it is done wrong, can have…catastrophic consequences."

"Not so far. We're doing pretty good."

"You are not hearing me, Jeff."

"What aren't I hearing, *Danny*?"

Danny leaned back. Jeff couldn't tell if he was exasperated or simply searching for another analogy. "The method must be done with attention to many different dimensions. The universe is like a giant, infinitely complex tapestry. If you pull one thread in the wrong direction, you can cause it to unravel."

"I can unravel the universe."

"Yes. You must abandon your attempts at…performing the method."

"Why do you keep saying, 'the method.' Isn't there a word for it?"

"Not in your language. Not in any language mere humans could understand."

"*Mere* humans? What does that mean?"

Danny's lip quirked slightly. "What are you calling it— the method?"

"Squashing."

Danny's brow furrowed, obviously trying to get his head around the implications of the word. "That is most inelegant."

"I agree."

"It is a most inaccurate descriptor of the method."

"Probably. But it's the word that leaped to mind when I was trying to explain it."

"Now we are even more concerned."

Jeff laughed. "Was that a joke? Because your comedic timing was pretty good."

Danny's face became severe. "Please do not think that this is humorous. We are not joking. We are…terrified."

"Terrified? Why?"

"Again, I think you are not hearing us."

"I'm hearing you fine. Don't tug on the carpet. I get it. But you guys do it all the time."

"We do. We understand how to do it properly."

"Okay. If you don't want me to do it wrong, teach me how to do it right."

Danny waved this suggestion away. Jeff wasn't sure whether he should feel insulted or not.

"This cannot happen," Danny said. "The fact that you can do it at all is of grave concern to us. You must cease immediately."

"I *must*?" Jeff asked.

"You must."

Jeff blinked, and Danny was gone.

JO WATCHED the viewscreen in horror as it panned over the battlefield, randomly zooming in on the Deseret fleet. Every ship she could see was literally swarming with Prox. From their distance, it looked as if each of them were crawling with ants—hungry, metal-eating ants. It was not, she realized, an analogy that was far off the mark.

"Receiving distress calls from fifteen of the Deseret ships, sir," Lieutenant Frey said.

"I don't doubt it," Jo said. She felt momentarily torn between continuing the attack or rescuing what she could of the Deseret crews. And what would she do if she did rescue them? Run? Get them to safety? Where was that? Back to earth? Back to Deseret, a planet on the verge of being picked clean by alien scavengers just as New Manila was? *No no no,* she thought. *I know my job. My job is war.*

"Course locked in, sir," Fin said.

"Take us in, Lieutenant."

The stars blurred for a moment as they sped forward toward the melee. They rushed directly toward the damaged Prox ship, at such velocity Jo was sure they were about to collide. At the last possible moment, however, Fin pulled up and away. The stars on their display careened in their course as the *Essex* banked and blasted away.

"Torpedoes on target," Raj said. "Impact in 2, 1."

Light engulfed the viewscreen again as the nuclear warheads detonated, sending scraps of the invading vessel soaring in all directions. "Raj, what kind of damage did we just do?"

Raj's fingers flew over his controls, and he looked from one display to another. "Their superstructure is losing integrity. It's breaking up, Captain."

"Thank God," Jo said. "At least we know now that they *can* be beat." She swiveled in her seat. "Mr. Frey, send a message to all capable ships to discharge another coordinated round of nukes at the lead ship."

Frey worked her own station, but quickly responded. "There are only three capable ships left, Captain, and one moon base. None of them are answering hails."

"Send the order just the same, firing mark in 45 seconds.

Mr. Fin, bring us on a course to add our firepower to theirs without taking on any friendly fire."

"How am I—?"

"I don't care. Just do it."

Fin gulped and nodded, looking up to check a chart. Jo noticed he was sweating. *Well, if ever there were a time,* she thought.

The stars on the viewscreen spun as Fin moved them into position and Raj counted down the attack. At one, he launched the torpedo and Fin piloted them away from the enemy ships again. "How many launched, number one?"

Raj's face fell. "Just ours, sir."

"Damage?"

"Minimal. Their shields absorbed the bulk of it without affect."

"Shit. How many can we launch at once?"

"Three. Which we just…sir, Prox soldiers approaching."

"Laser cannons, Weaponer."

"No good, sir. They're too close. We'd shoot ourselves."

"How many?"

"Thirty-five, with…457 close behind. Make that 650 and counting." Raj's voice was pitched higher than usual, but remained even. "The first of them is going to land on us in five, four, three…"

"I want a visual, Mr. Frey."

"Yes, sir."

The viewscreen changed to an exterior camera. They watched as a massive Prox soldier floated into view. Its six legs spun in free space until it reached out toward the hull. Jo heard the impact above her own head…followed by more, and more, and—it reminded her of popcorn popping, only deeper and more metallic.

She turned toward Laru. "Chief Engineer, deploy the electric fence."

"Deploying the fence, sir."

Jo watched the viewscreen and fought against her own anxiety.

"Fence employed."

Jo expected to hear something—maybe a sound like frying bacon—but there was nothing. She did exhale in pronounced relief to see every one of the Prox clinging onto their hull recoil, their legs lifting off the hull in a quick jerk of pain. A smile broke out over Jo's face. She had to stop herself from jumping up and down. "It worked!" she said in Laru's direction.

"Yes, sir, it—" he stopped when all heard the thumping above them resume.

"Mr. Laru, did you keep it on?"

"No sir. We can only do short bursts."

Jo unconsciously ran her fingers through her hair, caught at it and pulled until it hurt, thinking. "Okay, we don't know how many times that's going to work. Let's make the best of it. Mr. Fin, on my mark, get us out of here. Push the C-drive as fast as she'll go."

"Destination?"

"Away."

"Once more with the fence, Mr. Laru."

Once more she saw the Prox recoil, but not as far this time. "Go! Go! For fuck's sake, get us out of here!"

Fin punched it, and Jo was grateful they were all strapped in as the g-forces slammed them. A moment later, the inertial dampeners kicked in and the pressure eased. Jo looked up at the viewscreen, stifling a wail of relief when she saw that they'd got away without any of the deadly scavengers still holding onto the hull.

Weaponer Raj turned to face her. "Sir, we cannot just run."

"No, we can't. This is a tactical retreat."

Satisfied, he turned back to his controls. "That is all right, then."

Did he just question her authority in front of the crew? She wasn't entirely sure. More likely he was simply saying aloud what everyone was thinking. Fin turned to face her. "We're well away, sir. No sign of being followed."

"Mr. Frey, any sign of pursuit on your end?"

"None sir. All I'm getting is distress calls. But those are... dying out."

"Send a message to the approaching CDF fleet to hold back .5 parsecs from Deseret to await new orders. Send a summary by ansible to CDF HQ. Let them know what's happened here." She turned to Raj. "What were you able to glean about their shields, number one?"

"Almost impenetrable, sir. No obvious openings or vulnerabilities."

"If you had to guess at a weak spot, what would it be?"

"The engines, sir, almost certainly. I noted they were careful to keep them behind them. Their weapons batteries were always facing toward the enemy—toward us, sir. You'd expect that, of course, but there were a lot of us coming at them from all sides. I was trying to decide if they were positioning themselves offensively—bringing the maximum number of weapons to bear, or defensively—keeping the engines out of the line of fire."

"And which is it?" Jo asked.

Raj shook his head. "Impossible to tell, Captain."

Jo raised her fingers toward her lips, but stopped when she noticed blood on them. Only then did they really hurt. "Damn," she said quietly.

"Sir?"

"It's nothing…Listen up, everyone." She waited until all eyes were on her. "We can't win out there today. They beat us." She saw Fin look away. She noted the way that their tense shoulders slumped all around the room at her words. She leaned forward and held her hand up. The motion caught everyone's eye again. "But we're sure as *fuck* going to make a couple of stabs in the dark before we head home."

JEFF WANDERED SOL STATION, not really knowing what he was doing or where he was going. His brain buzzed. He didn't know how he got there, but he found himself staring out the large port glass at where the *Bohr* was docked. Then he heard yelling.

The sound jerked him out of his reverie, and he jogged toward the sound of it. As he got closer he realized it was not the sound of someone in distress, but in considerable frustration. He rounded a corner and continued to follow it down the hall, realizing he recognized the voice—had *dreamed* about the voice. He entered the room from which the voice issued and hovered in the doorway as he assessed the situation.

Dr. Stewart—Emma—was reaming out one of the technicians. Jeff gauged how long it had taken him from the first eruption of her ire to the present moment and was impressed that she had been yelling for nearly thirty seconds. He leaned in the doorway and crossed his arms. She had not yet seen him.

She was looming over a piece of equipment, and over two engineering techs flat on their backs, squirming to find access to the wiring. "The rhonda capillaries connect to the C ports, not the E ports, you idiots!" she tugged at her own hair. "Do you want to fry the terminator board?"

That's when she saw him. He waggled his fingers at her and gave her a sad—hopefully sympathetic—smile. She looked at her shoes and shook her head. Then she sighed and shuffled over to him. She looked like she hadn't slept in a week.

"I was going to ask how it's going," he began, "but…uh…"

"Yeah." She pitched her forehead forward against his shoulder. Jeff blinked. Did she really just do that? It was the most intimate gesture she had ever made toward him. He knew she had been warming up to him during their work together. Her smiles lasted a little longer every time they saw each other, and the small talk had been progressing toward playful banter. He enjoyed that. A little hesitantly, he put one arm around her shoulder and gave it a quick squeeze. "You would not believe the difficulty I've had getting—" she stopped herself mid-sentence, and Jeff realized she was about to say something about the techs in their hearing, but wisely thought better of it.

"Buy you a drink?" he asked.

"No, I…" she made the universal hand swoop indicating way too much work. "Fuck it. It's lunchtime."

"A three-martini lunch?"

"A what?"

"It's…I read old paperbacks. It's a hobby. And a three-martini lunch was…a thing at one time. But you lead the way. I'll follow. I'll even pay."

She grinned at that. No one in the military paid for anything. She turned toward the techs. "I'll be back in an hour—tops." She shot a warning look at Jeff. He raised one eyebrow. "When I get back I want to see that engine up and running." She tugged at his sleeve and almost ran into the hallway.

She held her hand to her mouth until they were out of earshot, then she started in. "Where the fuck does Jennings find these people?"

"What, the techs?"

"And why do we call them 'techs' if they can't tech their way out of a plastic bag? I swear to God, Jeff, I have to watch every fucking moment or they do it wrong."

"They're grunts, Emma. They know how to wire a star-ship. They don't know what you're trying to do or how to do it. They've never seen the equipment you're installing. Did you even give them the schematics?"

"Oh, sure, take their side."

"I'm not taking anyone's side. I'm just saying they're really good at what they do, and you're asking them to do something else. You might want to cut them some slack. And an even better idea is to give them the tools they need—like the schematics—so that they know enough about what they're doing to do it well."

Emma stopped and faced him. "That sounds like the voice of a man used to leading people and knowing how to get the best out of them."

"They don't call me captain for nothing."

She took his arm and rested her head on his shoulder as they walked. "I'm a bad captain."

He put his right arm around her. It felt good. He instantly felt his pulse rise and his erection stir. "Not *being* a captain, that's not really an indictment."

"Jeff, how do you do it?"

"Do what?"

"Captain." She said it as a verb. *How do you captain?*

"Pretty poorly, actually. I got everyone in my platoon killed. Everyone but me."

"I heard about that. It's why you like solo assignments."

He didn't answer at first. Then he said, "It's not something I like to talk about."

Thinking about Catskill caused his amorous feelings to sour. He dropped his arm. She noticed.

"Jeff, are you all right?"

"I'm…you know what? I'm…I'm pretty…I'm concerned."

She looked up at him and frowned. "About what?"

"You know, I wasn't…I wasn't going to tell anyone about this, but…I'm afraid you'll think I'm crazy."

"Try me."

"I saw Danny again."

"Danny?"

"My friend. He was killed at Catskill."

Emma nodded. "I remember you saying that the Ulim appeared to you…using his form."

"Yeah."

"And did they visit you again?"

He looked down. Then he met her eyes. "Yeah."

She grabbed his hand and jerked him in the opposite direction.

"What are you doing?"

"Taking you to see Jennings. Now."

"But—"

"You can't fuck around with this, Jeff. If you've been visited by the Ulim, it isn't just a private thing between you and them. This concerns all of us, and Jennings needs to know about it."

He didn't protest, because he didn't disagree. She was right. Of course she was. He'd just been in too much shock to see his proper course of action. It *had* seemed private. But it wasn't, not really.

He thought she would lead him to Jennings' office, but she obviously knew more than he did. That wasn't surprising —she was working closely with Jennings while he was playing solitaire and drinking whiskey. He wallowed in the feeling of being a worthless fuck for about thirty seconds. Then he let it go.

Emma had led him to the far side of the dock where the *Bohr* was moored. She approached an airlock and fitted her eye to the retina scanner. It identified her positively; then Jeff did the same. A moment later the lock slid open and she pulled him into it. Once through, she led him to a chamber with high rubber walls just like the one in Alberta, except that one side opened onto a viewing port where he clearly saw the *Bohr*, docked and still undergoing refitting.

In the middle of the chamber was a chair, again much like the one in Alberta, but not exactly the same. Jennings was leaning over it, listening to a tech explain something about its operation. Emma cleared her throat, and Jennings' head swiveled. Catching sight of them he gave a quick nod of acknowledgment, while continuing to listen. He asked a quick question of the tech and listened to the explanation. Then he clapped the tech on the back and said, "You let me know."

The man nodded, and Jennings walked over to greet them, extending his hand to Jeff. Jeff took it and was put at ease by its confident strength. "Admiral."

"Captain. Doctor." Jennings was all business. "Good timing—I was about to call for you. I've got news—just came over my neural. It hasn't hit the feeds yet. HQ is holding it back until we know more, but…"

Jeff's shoulders sagged. "Deseret."

"Yeah."

Jeff felt at his jaw. "It didn't go well?"

Jennings looked down and shook his head. "From all reports—and there were a lot of them—Deseret has been utterly gutted."

Despite thirty years of military training, Jeff reached out and grabbed his superior officer by the forearm. "And Jo?" He instantly regretted it—his failure of protocol, his use of her first name, the wavering note of hysteria in his voice.

To his great relief, Jennings placed both his big beefy hands on Jeff's shoulders and held them firmly, addressing him in the same spirit. "It's hard to say, Jeff. Last we heard from her she was in the thick of the battle. And as of five minutes ago—the last time I checked—we were still receiving ansible transmissions from the *Essex*. I can't say what *will* happen, but I know she's alive now."

Jeff looked over and saw a complicated range of emotions playing out on Emma's face—relief...and a flash of jealousy? Perhaps he had imagined it, or had simply wanted to see it. "But Deseret," Jeff breathed. "How many?"

"Nearly 250 million people." Jennings lowered his hands and turned to include Emma in the conversation. "I've got unqualified support from the civilian authorities for this project now. We're not just getting a trickle of CDF R&D funding now—we've got an unlimited commitment. Dr. Stewart, you order whatever obscure appliances you need to make this work. We're not pinching pennies anymore. Everyone sees this as our best chance to get troops where we need them *when* we need them. They've passed along one request—that you teach someone else how to do...whatever you do."

"I wish I could, Admiral, but—"

"Let me show you your new throne." Jennings cut him off

and led him over to the chair. "We're going to upload a patch to your neural that will feed all the vital statistics we need without additional wires sticking out of you. You'll also be able to monitor the *Bohr*'s location and how much power you're drawing—straight through the neural, no control panels. This should give you more control over your jumps."

"That's not why we're here," Emma said.

Jennings jerked up, surprised.

"Jeff's had a...visitation."

"Visitation?"

Jeff took a deep breath and nodded.

Jennings turned to the tech. "Excuse me a minute, Engineer Hsi. We need the room."

The young man's eyebrows rose, but he gave a quick nod and exited without comment. When the door slid shut, Jennings leaned against the massive chair in the center of the room and crossed his arms. "Captain?"

Jeff wasn't sure how to begin. "I was drinking, and—"

"Always a fine start to a story," Jennings tossed to Emma. She pursed her lips and did not smile. "Sorry, son. Continue."

"And the next thing I knew, Danny was in the room."

"Daniel Hightower? *Dead* Daniel Hightower?"

"Yes. If you'll recall, it's how they spoke to me before."

Jennings dropped his arms and stood up. "The Ulim."

"Yes."

"Came here?"

"Yes sir."

"There was an alien invasion of a CDF station and I'm only hearing about it *how long* after the fact?" Jennings looked alarmed, but there was outrage in his voice.

"To be honest, sir, I wasn't sure it was real."

Jennings bunched his eyebrows in confusion. "What do you mean?"

"We   had   this   conversation,   and   then   he just...*disappeared*."

"Disappeared."

"He was there one minute, warning me, and the next he was gone."

Jennings looked him straight in the eye, and Jeff could tell he was gauging his veracity. "And just what did you talk about?"

"He told me not to squash space, that I didn't know what I was doing. And that I needed to stop doing it—immediately and completely."

"And you said...?"

"I tried to reason with him, sir."

"And?"

"He wasn't having any of it." Jeff looked down, as if he had somehow failed.

"Assuming this wasn't just the whiskey talking—"

"How did you know it was whiskey, sir?"

Jennings gave him an *Are you kidding me?* smirk and continued. "Why do you think they want you to stop...squashing?"

"He said they are afraid, that it was dangerous."

"*They* are afraid?"

"Yes sir."

"What are they afraid of?"

"They said I could...unravel the universe."

Jennings laughed. "Really now? That's a bit dramatic, don't you think?"

"I...I don't know *what* to think, sir." Jeff suddenly felt thirty years younger, as if he were a cadet being called on the carpet.

"I think it's a lot more likely that they just don't want the competition."

"Competition for what?" Emma asked. Jennings looked surprised at the question, as if he had forgotten she was there.

"For trade, for power, for the domination of vast regions of space—for whatever their people might mutually *want*."

"And what do they want?" Emma asked.

Jennings looked to Jeff for an answer, but he didn't have one. "They're so different from us, sir. I couldn't even harbor a guess. My impression was that they just want to be left alone."

"Yes, but for what?" Jennings sighed. "Well…fortunately, this decision is mine, not yours. I'll take this…warning… under advisement. In the meantime, let's step it up. We need this project up and running yesterday now that Deseret has fallen."

"But sir, I—"

Jennings held up his hand. "We can always pull the plug at the last minute. In the meantime, let's get everything operational. Because when we need it, when we *truly* need it, we won't have a choice."

"NAVIGATION, I want you to chart a course to bring us in just behind the supporting Prox vessel—that way we won't be in sight of anyone's guns."

Fin sat up straight, then turned to face her. "But sir, how do we—"

"We come in dark, Mr. Fin. That's how we avoid detection. Get us moving on the exact coordinates we need to get into position to take a shot at their engines. Then, before we're in scanning range, shut down all power, including emergency power. We're a cold, dark, fast piece of driftwood and nothing more. Catch the vision, Mr. Fin?"

"I've got it, sir."

"Mr. Laru, how long will it take us to get back up to power so we can get off a shot at those engines?"

"Too long, sir," Laru said. His wild shock of blue hair was almost incandescent in the emergency lighting. "It will take 7.5 seconds for a complete reboot. I suggest keeping navigation and weapons systems on. We'll still be virtually undetectable. But we'll also be without shields."

"I'm aware of that risk, and I'm prepared to take it." She gave a curt nod. "It's a good idea. Let's do it. Mr. Raj, prepare to launch three thermonuclear devices—the biggest and baddest we've got. Mr. Fin, take us in as fast as we dare. Mr. Frey, complete radio silence, please. Mr. Laru—rig for silent running."

She watched the stars whirl on the main viewscreen as the *Essex* came about, then blur as she found her cruising speed. "Going dark, sir," Laru said. "Navigation and weapons systems blanketed and quiet."

A moment later, the overhead lights went out. The low incandescent glow of the emergency lighting and the flickering control panels provided just enough light to move around the bridge without bumping into anything.

"Course locked in," Fin's voice announced. "We're driftwood, sir."

"Mr. Frey, all decks, please."

"All decks ready, sir."

"This is your captain. From here on out we're running silent. I want all personal communication devices off. I want all neurals in sleep mode. I want nothing above a whisper. Don't drop a wrench, don't shriek if you cut yourself. We are running silent and that means *silent*. We don't know what the Prox can perceive and what they can't, so we're not going to give them anything *to* perceive. I know you are rehearsed, I know you are ready. Everything in your career has led you to this moment. We are either going to survive this run or we aren't. But one thing is clear—we're going to give it the best shot we've got. Captain Taylor, out."

Jo heard the last of the equipment whine into silence. She put her own neural on sleep and raised her upright index finger to her lips and made sure everyone saw her. *Shhhh.* Everyone nodded and glued their eyes to their controls. She was about to chew on a fingernail, but caught herself and stuffed her hand in her pocket.

It felt weird, running without a viewscreen. It was psychological, of course. The viewscreen wasn't a window, it was a monitor. But she still felt cut off from the space around her. She heard a thump on the outside hull, and she turned to Raj. "Prox?" she mouthed.

He shook his head, calm as ice. She nodded, realizing that with the shields down, they'd hear about it every time they hit a piece of rock. It was an extremely dangerous way to fly. If any of those rocks were big enough…

She dug her fingernails into the armrest of her command chair. She checked her straps. She also had to piss. No time for that now.

Fin waved his hand. Then he held up five fingers. Jo suddenly felt claustrophobic, as if the bridge were suddenly very small and very hot. She held her breath as, one by one, Fin withdrew his fingers until there was only one remaining in the air. That one, too, collapsed into his fist and Raj punched at his controls. He turned and whispered. "Torpedoes launched."

"Fin, get us out of here. Engage superlux!" Jo shouted, her voice sounding way too loud in the quiet deck.

It took two seconds for the C-drive to engage and when it

did, Jo felt like she'd hit a brick wall. She bore the full impact of the g-forces with gritted teeth and a muffled yowl of pain.

It took five seconds for the dampeners to engage, by which time she was sure she'd sustained a concussion. And if she had, then everyone had. Primary power resumed and the lights came back on. The ambient whine of the equipment resumed its normal levels. "Raj, did we pick up any passengers?" She unbuckled her restraint harness.

"None, sir," Raj said with a note of triumph.

"Frey, viewscreen, please."

The viewscreen flickered, then resolved, but she saw nothing but white. "What's wrong with it?" Jo demanded, swiveling toward her communications officer.

"Nothing's wrong with it, sir," Frey said, her hands flying over her controls. "It's really that bright out there."

"You're seeing the detonation, Captain," Raj said.

"Of our nukes?" Jo asked, confused. "They wouldn't be—"

"Of their engines," Raj interrupted her. And at that moment, she didn't mind his impertinence. Not one bit.

"Hot damn," she said, punching at the arm of her command chair in triumph. A moment later, cheers erupted from her crew. Fin stood up, his arms raised toward the ceiling. He started jumping up and down, making loud whooping noises. Frey crossed and planted a kiss on Raj's cheek. The Weaponer was still emotionless, but Jo noted he was blushing.

It was Chief Engineer Laru that called her back to reality. "Orders, sir?"

She'd been hugging Frey at that moment, but remembering herself, she straightened her uniform and returned to her chair.

"Hell, while our luck is holding, let's hit their other ship,"

Jo said, turning to Raj. "Weaponer, what's our arsenal looking like?"

"Sir, we're fine on lasers and particle cannons, but we're down to one nuke." Raj's face fell. "I'm sorry, Captain, but we don't have enough firepower to take out the last ship."

Jo nodded. "Okay. There's so much more I wish we could do. But we've done a lot, and we learned a lot. We know at least one way to beat these fuckers, and we have a lot more data that could lead us to other methods once we've analyzed it. We've wreaked enough vengeance and destruction for one day. Mr. Fin, take us home to Sol Station."

"Locking in a course now, sir."

"Mr. Laru, what's the best cruising speed you can give us?"

"We did C8.4 on the way out here, but it wasn't safe," Laru said. She found his long, horsy face compelling in the same way she found zoo animals fascinating. "The Corps of Engineers recommends C7 for this vessel."

"Do it."

"Mr. Frey, prepare a datapacket. Cram everything into it you can—every ounce of data, so that our strategic analysts can get a head start on it."

"On it, Captain."

She stood. "You have the con, Mr. Raj."

"Sir?" he lifted one eyebrow at her.

"I'll be back in five. I have to micturate like a race horse."

THE AIR in front of Admiral Jennings shimmered and a computerized voice broke the silence. "Ansible exchange request from Captain Joleen Taylor."

"Accept," Jennings said, swiveling to face the shimmer.

He rubbed at his eyes and tried to force himself to a full state of alertness.

The shimmering resolved into the form of Jo, hovering above his desk. "It's late, isn't it?" she said. "I can never keep the time difference straight. Sorry."

"It's alright, Captain," Jennings said. "I'd want to hear from you no matter what time it was. I'm relieved to be hearing from you at all."

"We got lucky," Jo said. Her features were grim.

"That may be, but I'm guessing good captaining had something to do with it, too," Jennings opined. "Tell me the story—short version first."

Jo brought him up to speed. "The datapacket should arrive at any moment."

As she was saying that, a light pinged in Jennings' neural. "Got it," he said. His impulse was to open it and sift through it while they were talking, but after what she'd just been through, she deserved his full attention. The fact is, he was a little in awe of her. "We'll have our techs pouring over every byte of data you sent, but even just your quick overview gives me hope," he said.

"We learned a lot, and I've got about a hundred ideas I want to try out in a simulator," Jo said.

"Right now I want you to get some sleep," Jennings said, feeling the need himself. "That's an order."

"Calling you was the last thing on my to-do list," she smiled. It was a tired smile.

"Call me again when you've caught eight hours and eaten something and we'll do the longer version."

"Affirmative. Before I sign off...how is Je—Captain Bowers?"

"Ornery, but you knew that," Jennings said. "I've transferred him and his team to Sol Station to begin tests with a spacefaring vessel."

"That must mean the scaling up has been successful?"

"Beyond our wildest dreams," Jennings affirmed. He considered telling her about the visit from the Ulim, but decided it could wait. No need to give her anything that might disturb her sleep.

"Tell me about the ship," Jo requested.

Jennings opened his mouth to complain that it was unimportant, but at the last moment indulged her. "It's a light research vessel, the *Bohr.*"

"Compliment?"

"Nine crew members and three science officers."

"When do you begin testing?"

"We should be ready in about..." he did some quick calculations in his head, "...three weeks, if we don't hit any snags."

"Good. That means we'll be back in time."

"You want to watch?"

"I want to do more than that," Jo said. She had that determined look that scared him a little. "You're going to need a captain for that thing."

CHAPTER SEVEN

J ennings had no sooner closed his eyes than he started
dreaming. At least, he thought he was dreaming. He
heard Becky's voice, so clear, even after all these years.
"You can't let him do it, Tom."

This strange dream had no visuals, only audio. Jennings
felt someone shaking him. "Wake up, sleepyhead."

He opened his eyes and started. Becky was sitting in the
chair near his desk, looking exactly as she had before her
illness had diminished her. Her hair shone gold in the dim
light of his cabin, and her smile was warm and all for him.

He sat up. *Am I dreaming?* he wondered. He punched his
leg. It hurt. *I don't think so.*

"What are you doing, you silly man? Oh, you think
you're asleep."

"No, I…"

She gave him that look that said, *You don't fool me for a
second.* "You're not dreaming. I'm really here."

"You can't be here. You're dead."

"No, we're really here. We're just not really *her.*"

"You're not Becky?"

"No. We borrowed her form to communicate with you. We thought it might get your attention."

"You're successful, then," Jennings said. Not an ounce of weariness remained in his bones. He felt electricity snapping in his brain. "Who are you?"

"We are the Ulim."

"I thought only Captain Bowers could see you."

"Only Captain Bowers has seen us. Until now. We appear to anyone we choose."

"And it's my turn."

"Captain Bowers has chosen not to heed us."

"Ah." Jennings sat upright and swung his feet onto the floor. He was wearing only his shorts, but Becky would not have minded. Weirdly, he didn't feel immodest even knowing that it *wasn't* really Becky beholding him in his glory. "That might have something to do with me."

"So we are appealing to you."

"Moving up the chain of command, eh?"

"It seems expedient."

"What do you expect me to do?" Jennings wondered how he could call for security without alerting the alien—or aliens. There was only one Becky before him, but he was unclear on the actual number of aliens involved in such a visitation. They did speak of themselves in the plural, after all.

"You must cease these experiments."

"Well, the thing is, we *need* these experiments."

"You must cease." The words sounded strangely stiff coming out of Becky's mouth. The real Becky would have said, "Knock it off, you jackass."

"Have you met the Prox?"

She cocked her head, as if searching for the word. She found it. "Ah, the species that destroyed your colony."

"Two of our colonies now, and a whole host of properties

in between."

"We know of them."

"They're killing machines. They've murdered millions of our people so far—many, many millions." He looked up at Becky to gauge her response. The real Becky would have put her hand to her mouth, her eyes would have widened, she might even have been sick from the horror of it. But this Becky looked as if he had reported on the weather. "They're moving toward our home world, and we don't know how to stop them."

"And you wish to survive." It was a statement.

"You're goddam right we wish to survive! What do you think?"

"If you wish to survive, you must find another way."

"You got any ideas?"

"We have not applied ourselves to your dilemma," she confessed. "It is not our place."

"You might want to try that before taking away the only chance we've got."

"Jeff Bowers is not the only chance you've got."

Jennings scowled. This was going nowhere. "Do you mind telling me what you have against us defending ourselves?"

"We do not begrudge you defending yourselves. We do not approve of the means."

"And why the hell not?" Jeff had told him about their objections. He just wanted to hear it from them.

"If you do not cease, we fear you will die."

"If we don't use him, I *know* we will die."

"But if you do not cease, we will die, too."

"This is the 'the universe is a carpet' thing, right?"

Becky looked momentarily confused. Then she smiled serenely. Yesterday, Jennings would have given his right nut to see that smile again. "Tapestry, we said. The universe is a tapestry."

"That's a difference of degree, not kind," Jennings smiled.

"You will stop?" Becky asked, giving him that look that promised sexual favors in exchange for a concession.

"No. I'm sorry, but no. We need every weapon in our arsenal."

"That is…unfortunate."

Jennings found her inhuman calm chilling. "So what do you plan to do?"

"You leave us little choice," she said.

ENSIGN ADI PENNER moved her limbs in slow motion as she drifted toward the bow of the *Bohr*. Her space suit was thick and awkward, but she had had enough practice doing repairs in space that she appeared to navigate nimbly into position. Reaching into the pack strapped to her abdomen, she drew forth a bottle of champagne and, with a minuscule puff of nav jets, turned back toward the viewing ports and held it aloft for all to see. In her earphones she heard a cacophony of cheers and whistles. A couple more puffs brought her face-to-face with the *Bohr* again. She concentrated on gripping the neck of the bottle in her thick gloves. It was awkward, but after a moment or two she was confident in her grasp. She drifted toward the bow of the research vessel, raised the bottle above the semi-globe of her helmet, and brought it down on the prow with all the force she could muster.

The bottle exploded, discharging shattered glass and foam in an expanding Rorschach pattern for all to behold and interpret for themselves. She had to turn down the volume in her helmet to save her hearing.

THERE WAS champagne inside as well. Jennings grabbed the elbow of an ensign passing with a tray of flutes and made sure that Jeff, Dr. Stewart, and Captain Taylor all had fresh glasses. "Admiral, I've had enough," Emma complained.

"Nonsense. You can curse me in the morning. Tonight we celebrate."

She narrowed one eye at him but accepted the champagne.

Looking around, Jeff saw Jason Tan talking with some techs. Tan noticed he was looking and waved. Jeff smiled and raised his glass.

"There's a lot of brass here," Jo noted. She pointed with her chin toward a cluster of admirals and captains near the makeshift bar.

"Morale has been pretty low around here since Deseret bit it," Jennings said, his voice quiet. He kept his smile on for appearances. He raised his glass at one of his fellow Admirals as she passed. "But between the launch of the *Bohr* tomorrow and the intel that you brought back from Deseret, we've got a one-two punch that is making folks feel...well, not just hopeful, but downright elated."

"It was looking pretty grim," Jo affirmed. "When we were watching the Prox dismantling the Deseret forces, I just kept thinking, 'There goes Earth.'"

"You're not the only one, Captain." Jennings took a swig of his champagne.

"How are we explaining this?" Jo asked. Jeff noted the bags under her eyes, and he wondered how long it had been since she'd gotten a full night's sleep.

"What do you mean?" Emma asked.

"I mean the *Bohr* launch. Jeff's…ability is top-secret. What do all these people *think* we're doing here?"

"Ah," Jennings nodded. "Three and four star Admirals are all read in—they've got the clearance. Everyone else thinks that Captain Bowers here discovered a new, alien technology that he brought back from New Manila."

"That's pretty much the truth," Jeff said, his eyebrows raised.

"Hew as close to the truth as you can, and the lies are easier to handle," Jennings agreed.

"A toast!" The cry came out of nowhere, but it was quickly taken up by many others, until the whole bay was chanting in unison, "Toast! Toast! Toast!"

"You're on, Admiral," Emma said, slipping away.

"Hey…" Jennings objected, but within moments he found himself standing alone with all eyes on him.

"Should have been you," Jo leaned over and whispered in Jeff's ear.

While she was speaking, his eyes caught Emma's and held them for a moment until she looked away. She buried her nose in her champagne flute and turned her back. "I'd sooner die," he answered. "This is why he gets paid the big credits."

Jennings raised a thick, red hand and held it up until the noise subsided. When it did, Jeff was amazed at how silent the room was. Everyone seemed to be holding their breath.

"This is a night that history will speak of," Jennings began. "A night when the timid dare to hope, and the brave gird their loins for battle."

A cheer went up. It was a hell of an opening, and not one that Jeff would ever have thought of. He wondered if Jennings had prepared it ahead of time or if he really was as confident and commanding as he seemed to be.

"New Manila caught us by surprise. Deseret dashed our hopes that we might turn back this alien scourge by conventional means. Tonight, however, we find ourselves poised between our recent defeat and our imminent victory."

Cheers again. People hooted and whistled and raised their glasses aloft.

"This is a pause. It is not really a celebration, for as yet we have not triumphed. But consider it a foretaste of that victory celebration we will soon enjoy. Consider it that moment before the trumpet blast when we secure the straps on our shields, draw a full breath into our lungs, revel in the warmth of the sun on our living bodies, take a final draught of sweet wine, and say to our comrades-at-arms, 'this day will bring us glory, it will bring glory to our people, and to our gods.'"

Cheers erupted again from the crowd, more frenzied than before.

"Is he quoting?" Jeff whispered.

"I have no clue," Jo answered.

"So drink up while they're still pouring the good stuff. Because the sack will rot your gullet." Laughs rocked the room. Jeff had no idea what "sack" was, and he wondered if anyone else did, either.

Jennings held his glass aloft and kept it there until quiet once again ruled the room. "A toast to Captain Jeff Bowers, the messenger of the gods, who went in search of wisdom and smuggled a weapon out of Olympus."

Suddenly every eye was on Jeff. They were cheering him. He smiled awkwardly and raised his glass sheepishly.

"And to Dr. Stewart and her team who have prepared the *Bohr* for our test tomorrow." There were more cheers, but they were subdued. The crowd was mostly military, Jeff noted, and there was a longstanding rivalry between the CDF and the CSC. "And finally, to the crew of the *Bohr*, who will be stepping courageously into the void. I give you her captain, Captain Joleen Taylor!"

Jeff's jaw dropped as the cheers exploded around him.

Jo grinned broadly and raised her glass in greeting to the crowd. When she had taken in the room, she lowered her eyes to meet Jeff's.

"I FORBID IT," Jeff said flatly.

"Not your call, Captain," Jennings said. He felt at his head. Too much champagne. He was going to regret this in the morning. Hell, he was beginning to regret it now.

"I won't do it," Jeff said.

"Sit down, Captain."

"I prefer to stand, sir."

"Sit *down*, Captain. That's an order."

Jeff sat. His lips were tight and grim. He blinked.

"You've got a soft spot for Captain Taylor. I get that. And that's exactly why we don't allow romantic entanglements among our officers."

"Yes, sir. But—"

"There ain't a reasonable 'but' on earth to that, so you just keep your mouth shut, son."

Jeff did.

"That ship needs a captain."

All ships did. Jeff did not dispute it.

"Taylor is one of our best."

"So don't risk her."

"Will she be at risk, Jeff? In your hands?"

"This is an experiment."

"So I should just put some greenhorn in the seat, because it doesn't matter if he dies, right?"

Jeff's jaw worked.

"What we need is our bravest." Jennings sighed, ran his fingers through what was left of his hair and leaned forward on his elbows. "Look, Captain, I'm going to level with you. I got you on one side saying, 'Don't you dare send her' and I got Taylor on the other side saying, 'Don't you dare send anyone else.' You ever tried arguing with Captain Taylor?"

Jeff looked down.

"Not a fight you're going to win, is it?"

Jeff shook his head.

"So what do you suggest I do?"

"You're the boss."

"That's right. And I'm putting my best captain in the seat. You're dismissed."

JEFF WASN'T happy about it, but he didn't have a choice. He put on his best game face as he made his way to the docking station, toward his rubber donut, toward the *Bohr*. Emma was there to meet him. "It's about time," she said, looking concerned.

"Let's do this," he said, throwing himself into the chair without ceremony.

Jennings stepped into the donut and scowled. "Everything okay here, Captain?"

"Everything's fine. We'll have him hooked up and ready to go in about two minutes."

"The crew has just finished their checklist. They're ready when you are."

Jeff nodded.

Jennings stepped up onto the riser where the chair was enthroned. He put a hand on Jeff's shoulder. "No hard feelings, son."

Jeff couldn't look at him. "None, sir."

Jennings' eyebrows rose. "I hope that's true." He nodded at Emma. "You take good care of him. Everything we are is riding on this."

"No pressure there, Admiral."

"Sorry about that. Reminding myself, more than anyone else, I guess."

Jeff knew the reminder was meant for him as well.

Dr. Tan entered swiftly and sat in a swivel chair to his right. "Just like old times, eh, Captain?"

"What do you need, Tan?"

"You can keep your shirt on. I just need access to your neural port."

Jeff raised his head a couple inches from the headrest and Tan plugged him in. He always expected to feel something when that happened, but he never did.

"I'm going to run a quick diagnostic, so you'll notice some interior sensations, but nothing uncomfortable. I just need to make sure all our wires are connecting."

Jeff nodded. He was used to this. For the next several minutes, he saw lights flashing in his peripheral vision, felt tingling in his limbs, heard buzzing in his ears, all in rapid succession.

"That's it, then." Tan placed a hand on his arm. "Good luck, Captain."

"Thank you, Doctor." He was surprised to find he meant it. Tan followed Jennings out.

Emma sat on the large chair next to him. He wanted to lean over and touch her lips to his. A part of him knew the gesture would not be unwelcome. But he also knew that he was facing a window facing the *Bohr*. Jo might not be watching, but she could be. He stayed where he was.

"You shut this down at any sign of trouble," she said.

"I know the drill."

"Draw as much energy as you need—"

"Em, I got this."

She nodded and swallowed. She placed her hand on his arm, too, just as Tan had done. But then she leaned down and planted a kiss on his cheek. Without waiting for a reaction, she turned and exited the donut.

"Shit," he said.

"What was that?" Jennings' voice emitted from the speaker next to Jeff's head.

"Nothing. It's just....*shit*, this is on."

"You got that right."

Jeff couldn't let himself be distracted by what Jo might or might not have seen. He didn't do it, after all. Hopefully that was clear. And besides, why should he care? Why didn't he just kiss Emma? What was he afraid of? Jo had made it abundantly clear that she was not girlfriend material. But Emma? Who knew what she wanted or would put up with? *It's worth exploring,* Jeff thought, *even if she's only 80% my type.*

"Focus," he told himself out loud.

He looked through the viewing port at the *Bohr*. There were twelve lives aboard that ship. And one of them was the woman that he had loved for most of his adult life. *How crazy am I?* he wondered. Suddenly the Ulim's warning echoed in his brain, and he marveled at his own hubris, his own foolhardiness.

"Captain, you make those astronauts wait any longer, they're going to want to come back aboard for lunch."

"Sorry, sir. Just...finding my focus."

"Look under the sofa."

"Thank you, sir." The corner of his mouth turned up in a smile and a bit of his anger toward Jennings dissipated.

He closed his eyes and called up a vision of the *Bohr* in his mind's eye. Then he reached out with his mind and took in the whole space station. He drew on the power supply they'd rigged for him. The feed was somehow brighter, crisper than the energy from the generator in Alberta. If anyone had asked him to describe it, he would say it was "quicker," but he'd be hard-pressed to explain what that meant. Instead he just fed from it, and he feasted well. He drew more, then more, reaching out further and further with his consciousness. He took in the earth—all of it, including the thoughts and feelings of all twelve billion sentient creatures there, along with the heavier animal and plant life. All of it was teeming, vibrant, alive.

But not as alive as he felt right now. He reached beyond earth to the Solar system. He drew more power and reached out toward Alpha Centauri. He embraced the yellow-orange star, feeling its radiation, its pulsing life. It suddenly occurred to him that he didn't need an artificial power source—once in the All, he could tap into any star in the universe. The power at his disposal was infinite.

He hadn't known exactly what he was going to do with the *Bohr* until just that moment, but now it was clear. He would put it into orbit around their neighbor star.

He raised his hands and gripped the space around Sol Station with one thumb and forefinger. With his other hand he grasped at the space surrounding the star. Then he simply ignored the space in between, invalidating it, nulling it, effectively bringing the fingers and thumbs of both hands together.

Then the energy he'd gathered erupted, twisted in on itself, and exploded.

CHAPTER EIGHT

J eff felt the vertigo of distanceless space rushing back into distance—like a localized big bang, his grasp failed and the elasticity of space exerted itself, resuming its former and natural state. A rubber band snapped with a sound that ended worlds.

He felt like he was falling, the energy no longer buoyant, but ripping through him like shards. He sat up, gasping for breath, clutching at the armrests of the great chair, his eyes wide but unseeing.

A moment later, his vision resolved, as did his hearing. The viewport in front of him was cracked and shock waves continued to roll through the station. The red alert signal was sounding, and emergency crews were rushing toward the cracking glass and spraying adhesive sealant over its surface.

Emma rushed in, followed by Tan and Jennings. She rushed to his side. "Are you all right?" she asked.

Jeff didn't answer. There was too much to take in. Jennings contented himself with a glance at Jeff, then he stood stock still, his eyes rolled up in his head, reading incoming reports on his neural.

"What happened?" Emma asked.

"I don't…I don't know."

"Oh, shit," Jennings said.

"What?" Jeff yelled in his direction. "What?"

Tan was by his side, now, unplugging his neural, preparing a dermal spray. Before Jeff could object, his vision dimmed and his panic was replaced by a cold, synthetic peace.

WHEN JEFF AWOKE AGAIN, it was dark. The only lights around him were blinking medical monitors. He raised his arm, feeling the drag of an IV in his arm.

"Look who's awake." The shadow of Dr. Tan leaned in the doorway.

"Tan," Jeff said in greeting. "What happened?"

"You suffered a severe concussion," he answered. "Although we can't figure out how."

"My head hurts," Jeff said.

"It should. Means you're normal and human."

"I feel like shit."

Bits and pieces of memory floated back to him. The grasping of space, bringing his hands together, the collapse of distance, the explosion.

Jeff jerked upright.

"Whoa there, Captain," Tan said. "You're under my orders now. You stay still or I'll sedate you again. That's a promise."

Jeff forced himself to lie back down. It wasn't hard since it hurt like hell to move.

He looked up and to his right, but nothing happened. They'd taken him offline.

"Please call the Admiral," Jeff said.

"It's the middle of the night."

"Call the Admiral or I'll rise up and snap your spine, you weaselly excuse for a man."

Tan blinked, frowning. Then he scowled. Then he looked up and to the right. "It's your funeral, tough guy," the doctor said. It was a perfect exit line, but he didn't leave.

———

JEFF MUST HAVE DRIFTED off again. He opened his eyes, his vision blurry. When it resolved, Admiral Jennings was sitting beside him, looking a little lost. Jeff smiled. "Reporting for duty, sir."

Jennings looked up and nodded. His face was friendly, but grim.

"What happened?"

"We were hoping you'd be able to tell us that, Captain."

"I don't know. I didn't do anything different. It just… slipped, guess."

"It slipped?"

"I guess."

"I was hoping for a bit more detail than that."

Jeff looked away. The memories were starting to congeal again.

"Jo?"

Jennings looked down. "Captain, there's no easy way to tell you this. And God knows I blame myself. And you're going to blame me too, no doubt. Uh…" he sighed, then met Jeff's eyes. "She's dead, Jeff. I'm so sorry. You can't know how sorry I am."

Jeff felt dizzy. It was a good thing he was already lying

down. He clutched at the bedclothes with both hands and struggled to sit up.

"No. Relax, Captain. That's an order. You're pretty beat up yourself."

Jeff eased his aching head back to the pillow. Through gritted teeth, he said, "She can't be..."

Jennings nodded. "But she is."

"And the crew?"

"All dead. And more."

"More?"

"I have no explanation for what happened. I'm just going to lay out what we found, and maybe you can make some sense of it, all right?"

Jeff nodded. He was holding his breath.

"After the explosion, we found that the *Bohr* was wrecked—"

"Where did you find it?"

"Right where it had been, visible from the viewport. It hadn't moved."

"But you say it was wrecked. How?"

"It looked like it collided with another ship. But the thing we can't figure out is...the ship it collided with was also the *Bohr*."

"What? I don't understand."

"Neither do we. What we got down in the dock right now are two ships, both called the *Bohr*, fused together into one massive lump of metal."

Jeff blinked.

"The mass of the wreckage is twice that of the original *Bohr*, before the...the accident. We can see some markings, but it's hard to tell what came from what. The ships appear to be identical, but again...it's just a lump of scrap metal now."

"And the crew? Jo?"

"We've found remains of fifteen people so far—we're collecting DNA."

"But there were only twelve aboard."

"Right. Jeff, it looks to us like whatever you did...it duplicated the *Bohr*, along with everyone inside. Then the original and the duplicate ship...it's like they tried to occupy the same space. And of course, they couldn't."

"But I didn't duplicate them...I mean, I didn't mean to..."

"I know you didn't mean to, son, but whatever you did... that's the effect it had. And there may be other explanations. We're open to any theories you might have."

Jeff tried to speak, but only sounds came out. His throat had swollen up with emotion and his eyes brimmed. "Jo..." was all he could manage.

Jennings placed his hand on Jeff's arm and squeezed it.

"I want you to rest, Captain. Heal. And I want you to go into your memory—into your imagination—and I want you to figure out what you did and why it had that effect. A lot of folks are urging me to give up on this, on you. But I still think what you're doing is one of our best hopes. We just got to figure out how to do it safely. I need you to figure that out, Captain. That's your mission."

Jeff nodded, but his nod was almost imperceptible as he stared straight ahead.

EMMA PAUSED at the door of Jeff's room. She knocked. He didn't look up. She entered anyway and sat on the side of his bed. She took his hand. "Hey, soldier," she said.

Only then did he look up. His head had stopped hurting. They had restored his neural. He'd been ignoring the messages from her.

"You're looking a lot better." She wasn't wrong. His appetite had returned, and so had his strength.

"Jeff, look at me."

He did. His face registered as much emotion as a slab of slate.

"We haven't talked about this, but we need to."

He betrayed nothing.

She pressed on. "I've had some feelings for you. I think that it was mutual."

He didn't deny it. He held her gaze. Slowly, he acknowledged her words with a nod.

"And I know you still had feelings for Jo…for Captain Taylor. At first I was jealous, but I've had some time to think after the accident. I know what it's like to carry a flame for someone that you know…well, that it's never going to be. That doesn't mean you stop loving them. It doesn't mean you should. And it doesn't mean you can't love another."

He nodded again. His eyes became glassy, but he blinked back the water.

"I know you loved her. And it's okay with me that you loved her. Hell…" she allowed herself a brief laugh. "I admit it, I was fond of her. I didn't want to be…but I was. I understand why you would fall so hard, for so long. She was…an amazing woman."

Jeff looked down, his resolve beginning to crumble.

"You need to mourn her. That's good and right and proper. I won't begrudge you that. Not for a second."

He opened his mouth to speak, but only a croak escaped. He closed it again.

"It's okay. You don't need to say anything. I think I understand it all. And…" she touched his chin and guided his eyes back to hers. "…I still have those feelings. I know it's a bad idea." She smiled. "And I don't care."

Jeff cleared his throat. "How can it matter?"

She sat up straight, a little shocked. "What do you mean?"

"The Prox are coming. They're still coming, aren't they?"

Emma nodded. "They're still coming."

"What damage have they done...since I've been here?"

"They took out the Indu Oasis."

"That's not a colony..."

"No, it's a space station. A joint Indian-Nepalese project."

"It's along the path, I take it? The path to earth."

"Yes. In a direct line."

He shook his head. "We're fucked. We're really and truly fucked."

Emma didn't disagree with him. "Jo discovered some strategies—"

"It won't be enough."

"Probably not, no."

"Emma...I like you. A lot. I could see us making a life together, after I retired. Which...wouldn't have been so far away. I didn't dare to hope, but I could see it happening. I *wanted* it to happen."

She squeezed his hand and smiled sadly.

"But I'm going to have a hard time sharing champagne while the world burns around us."

"I didn't ask you to do that."

"I know you didn't. I'm just putting that on the table. The way things are...I need to go down fighting. I can't be in two places at—" he stopped and looked into space.

"What? Jeff, what just happened?"

"Oh. Shit. I know what happened," he breathed.

"What happened to who?"

"What happened to the *Bohr*. To Jo. To everyone in that crew." He sat up straight, felt the screaming protest of his atrophied muscles. He swung his legs over the side and ripped at the IV in his arm.

"Jeff, stop. You're scaring me."

"I know why it did what it did." He stood shakily but steadied himself by putting his hands on her shoulders. He looked in her eyes. "And I know how to make sure it doesn't happen again."

THE PROX SWARMED over the space station. Four fighters made swooping passes near the carrier ships, firing blindly and wildly at every soldier and worker that they passed. The station itself had sixteen gunnery ports, all of them ablaze. Most of their shots connected. Every second, Prox soldiers went down. But their efforts didn't make a dent in the overwhelming numbers of Prox descending on them, dismantling them…eating them.

Admiral Jennings sighed and buried his head in his hands for a moment. Then he opened a different file and watched the entire battle play out from the perspective of a different camera.

He didn't know what he was looking for. He hoped that if he found it, he'd know it. But until then he simply kept replaying the battle over and over, each time hoping a different perspective would show him something—anything —about their enemy that he didn't already know. Something that would give him an idea, a strategy, or some hope.

Captain Taylor had given them much—for one thing, they knew the Prox carrier ships could be destroyed. That was huge. For another, Taylor had hit upon a strategy that worked against them. But the number of battle cruisers they had that could carry the kind of payload needed was limited. It might have worked if they'd been able to move them faster than C8…but that was out of the question now.

He poured himself a scotch and allowed himself to mourn the dream that Jeff Bowers had brought to him. It really had been too much to hope for. And the Ulim had been right— they didn't know what they were doing, and it had ended in tragedy.

He took a sip. It occurred to him that perhaps the Ulim had sabotaged the experiment. Perhaps it was a warning shot, of sorts. After all, they didn't really know what had happened. And he didn't trust the crystalline aliens—why should he?

A message pinged in his neural. He slammed his glass down and swore. Then he looked up and accessed it. It was from Command Intelligence.

—Distress call from Danforth Station. Prox attack.

Jennings blinked. He had an idea where Danforth station was, but he couldn't pinpoint it on a map. Maybe he was wrong. He had to be. He pulled up the stellar cartography interface and did a quick search. Danforth Station, a commercial research and development outpost near Epsilon Indi was… Jennings felt a chill run through him. It was on the other side of the galaxy from New Manila. His hands started shaking and he gripped his scotch and knocked the rest of it back. It could only mean one thing—the Prox were making for Earth from two different directions. "We're fucked," he said out loud. *It's all over but the cyanide capsules*, he thought.

He poured himself another scotch, spilling a little when the door signaled a request for entry. Why hadn't Liu told him? He'd ask later. He put his hands under his desk and said, "Come."

The door slid open, and Captain Bowers limped in, supported by Dr. Stewart.

"Captain, what in hell's—"

"I know what happened."

"What?"

"To the *Bohr*. I know why the…accident…why it happened. And I can prevent it from happening again."

A flicker of hope fluttered in Jennings' breast. He dared not indulge it.

"Sit, damn you, before you fall and break one of my antiques. They're worth more than you are."

Jeff smiled at that, and Emma helped him to a chair directly facing the Admiral's desk.

"Now tell me what you *think* you know."

"When I grabbed the two ends of space—"

"I will never get used to this language."

"It's not scientific, I'll grant you," Jeff acknowledged.

"Just…continue."

"When I grabbed the two ends of space, I saw the *Bohr* where it was, and, in my mind's eye, I saw it where I wanted it to be. I saw it in two different places at once. When I let go—"

"Are you telling me that the mere act of your imagining the *Bohr* in a new space replicated the ship and everything aboard it?"

"I think so, yes. And when I squashed space—"

"The two ships collided," Jennings finished his sentence.

"Exactly."

"That's the steamiest pile of horse shit I've ever heard in my life."

"And yet, I'll bet my life that it's the truth."

"How come this never happened before?"

"Because before, I didn't see the object in two places, I

only saw it where it was, and then imagined squashing the space."

"Then why the hell did you do it differently this time?"

Jeff blinked. "I...I don't have an answer for that, Admiral. I just...did. It was bigger, it was...there was more pressure. I was improvising. I thought..."

"And you were wrong."

"I was wrong." Jeff looked down. "This is all on me. Again. It's Catskill all over again."

"Captain, I forbid you to go there."

Jeff ignored him. "And if we don't get back on track, this, and Catskill...it's all going to look like small potatoes compared..." he didn't finish his sentence.

Jennings got it. "Son, you cannot blame yourself for the demise of the human race."

Jeff bit his lip. "Why not?"

"Because it hasn't happened yet. And we're sure as fuck not going down without a fight."

CHAPTER NINE

There were more than 8,000 people on Sol Station, and the hangar would only hold about half that number. Nevertheless, it seemed to Jennings that the whole population had squeezed together to be there. *God help us if there's some kind of incident,* he thought. *The stampede would kill more than the incident itself.* He was confident that whoever wasn't physically there was watching via their neurals or pads or viewscreens. He looked up and connected to the public address system in his own neural.

"We lost some battles. We didn't lose the war. Not yet. Not by a long shot. And God help us, not ever."

There was a murmur of defiant agreement.

"One of those battles was the loss of the *Bohr*. We lost a lot of fine people that day." Jennings stole a glance at Captain Bowers and saw him staring at his shoes. "As with every weapon, you get it wrong before you get it right." He paused and noted the dead, dreadful silence in the hangar. "I just received new intelligence that the Prox are coming at us from another direction as well." He watched their eyes widen, waited for the roar of surprise and dismay to decay. Then he continued. "The need for the ability to move our fleet quickly and efficiently has never been more acute than it is right now. So we need to get this right. We need to try again." He let that sink in a moment. "We're outfitting a new vessel for that test, the *Kepler*. It's structurally identical to the *Bohr*, so we'll know that if we get it right this time, then it's about our technology, not about the ship."

There was a buzz of whispers and commentary. He raised his hands to quiet the crowd. "I know this seems risky. It is. But we need to try again because if we don't, we don't stand a chance against the Prox."

Jennings saw heads nodding at that. No one was blind to the threat that faced them. "But I'm not going to bullshit you. It's dangerous. What happened to Captain Taylor and her crew could happen again...and again." He purposely did not look at Jeff, didn't want to see his protesting glare. "And because of that I can't order anyone onto the *Kepler*. That's not how you make heroes. Heroes aren't made by compulsion, but by self-sacrifice, by brave women and men who don't hesitate to put themselves in harm's way because they're soldiers, and that's what soldiers do. They don't hesitate because they know that there is something at stake that's bigger than themselves." He stopped and listened to the echo of his voice fade. He circled slowly, looking into the eyes of those in the first row.

"Earth needs some heroes today. Who among you has the guts to volunteer for the *Kepler*?"

He kept eye contact with people as he fell silent. He expected a few brave souls to step forward. He wasn't expecting Bowers.

Jeff took three steps forward and stood at attention. "Captain Jeffrey Bowers, reporting for duty, sir. I will command the *Kepler*."

Jennings opened his mouth to swear at him, but closed it again. He understood. Bowers wasn't about to let anyone else go under for his mistake, not unless he was on the line, too. *But he's too great an asset to allow the risk,* he thought. Another voice in his head said, *And if you don't let him take that risk, he'll clam up on you. He'll be no good to you at all.* That was probably right. And a captain stepping forward was a good start. Jennings nodded.

"A captain needs a crew," he shouted.

Dr. Emma Stewart stepped forward to stand with Bowers.

"Oh, Christ," Jennings said, unfortunately out loud. The rest of Stewart's team took a step forward as well.

A pilot stepped up next. Then a weaponer. Within seconds the *Kepler* had a full complement.

"It's good to see the human race still breeds heroes," Jennings said. "Training on board the *Kepler* will begin at 0700 hours. Thank you all for your time, your attention, and your prayers—we're going to need them. Dismissed."

Jennings terminated the neural link to the public address system as he strode over to Bowers and Stewart and the rest of the crew that had assembled. But his words were for Jeff alone. "That was reckless, and you put me on the spot."

Jeff said nothing. Emma cleared her throat. "Looks like we're putting all our eggs in this basket, then."

"It sure the hell looks like it," Jennings barked.

"It's a damn fine basket." Jeff offered a weak smile.

"It damn well better be."

JENNINGS RAISED A GLASS, and the conversation died down. Jeff shifted in his seat, just wishing the evening was over. He'd been hosted in Admirals' dining rooms before, but rarely, and he felt keenly out of place. Emma sat beside him, and despite her best efforts at maintaining professional decorum, tongues were starting to wag.

"This is the best wine on Sol Station," Jennings held his glass up to the dim light, softened for atmosphere. "As for dinner, we flew the head chef at Chez Panisse in Vancouver here to prepare it, and I, for one, cannot wait. Is that extravagant?" He paused for effect. "You're damn right it is. It is, in a way, what we're fighting for. Not wealth or privilege, but something that is as old as our species—conviviality, celebration, the company of friends. I want you all to look around the table tonight," Jennings said, his features growing a bit graver. "This gathering—this *kind* of gathering—is precisely what our enemy seeks to steal from us. Not only existence, but the joy of living, the love of friends, the communion of human souls. Let us enjoy this meal as a symbol for everything we seek to preserve. Let us enjoy it consciously, deliberately, completely." He took a slow sip of his wine, smiled his satisfaction, and returned his glass to the table. "Now who can I pour for?"

There was a general burst of enthusiastic hubbub around the table as people raised their glasses and murmured approvingly.

"He's very good at this sort of thing," Emma whispered.

"Jennings?" Jeff said. "All I heard was, 'Eat, drink, and be merry—for tomorrow we die.'"

"Were you always like this?" Emma asked.

Jeff stared into his glass. After what seemed like minutes, he finally answered. "No. Not always."

Emma sighed and nudged his feet with hers under the table. "Sorry. I don't always think," he confessed.

"That's the human condition."

"Captain Bowers," a voice called across the table. Jeff

looked up to see Dr. Osprey, the psychologist. "Do you feel ready for this?"

Jeff shifted in his seat again, but he was writhing inside. "I've never been more ready, Doctor."

"I'm a little out of the loop. How did the tests go? Are you able to move yourself?"

"I have successfully teleported myself to earth and back. I've got the technique down."

"But you had the technique down before—for just moving the ship, didn't you?"

Jeff blinked, his face hard and immovable. *He's fucking with me,* Jeff thought. *He wants to see if I'll crack.* He wondered if Jennings had put him up to this. Probably. "I did. And then I improvised. That was a grave error. It won't happen again."

"Isn't this all improvisation? I mean, there aren't any instruction manuals for what you're doing." Osprey held his gaze. Jeff wanted to rip the man's ridiculous mustache off his face.

"It is, the first time. And then I do it again. And again. Then it's routine, it's protocol."

"But it's only routine when you don't deviate from your protocol."

"I'm not sure what you're fishing for, Doctor," Jeff said, as patiently as he could. "Are you trying to say, 'Don't fuck up tomorrow,' in which case you're being an asshole? Or are you intentionally trying to provoke me in order to gauge my emotional stability, in which case you are also being an asshole?"

Osprey didn't blink, but a humorless smile seeped from one side of his lips to the other. A frosty silence had descended on Jeff's end of the table, and everyone suddenly found their wine glasses profoundly interesting.

"Good luck tomorrow," Osprey said.

Jeff gave him a curt nod and then turned to Emma. "Prick," he whispered. He didn't care who heard.

"He's just doing his job."

Jeff waited until the conversations started up again. "I don't think much of his job."

"Psychologists get that a lot."

Jeff grunted.

"Captain," a woman about Jeff's own age got his attention. He welcomed the change. "How far will you be taking the *Kepler* out tomorrow? Before the test?"

Jeff noted from the woman's uniform that she was from the Colonial Press Corps. Of course they would be here.

"About 500,000 kilometers."

"In which direction?"

"Away from anything with people on it."

She grinned at that. He grinned back.

"Most people think that's for safety," she said, but Jeff heard the implied question.

"Most people would be right. There's no danger, but we're going to get some distance, just so no one worries."

"And by 'no one' you mean the brass?"

"I probably do."

"But you don't think it's necessary?"

He saw what she was trying to do, and he moved to shut her down. "I think it's prudent."

"Prudent..." she said the word as if it were wine, tasting it on her lips. "That's a pretty old-fashioned word."

"I'm an old-fashioned guy."

"What makes you old-fashioned?"

Jeff watched her face. She was looking for some angle, something to make a routine story about an important test pop.

He looked over at Emma and saw her looking at him. She was waiting for his answer, too. He looked across the table. Osprey was watching him like a hawk.

"It's not very popular these days," he began, "but the reptilian brain is still part of who we are. It's territorial. It's aggressive. It doesn't tolerate assholes." He narrowed one eye at the reporter. "And it doesn't like to lose."

JEFF WAS ABOUT to turn in when he heard a knock on his cabin door. *An old-fashioned knock*, he thought. *Quaint.* He touched the button on the wall and the door slid open. "Emma," he said.

She was leaning against the doorframe with a wry smile that betrayed not enough sleep and a bit too much alcohol. "Jeff."

"Come in," he said.

She didn't hesitate. She slunk into his room and sat on his bed. She started taking off her left shoe.

"Um…Emma, what are you doing?"

"Sneaking up on you," she said, dropping her right shoe.

Jeff chuckled and leaned against the wall. "I think you're a little tipsy."

"I feel fucking *great*."

"You need to get some sleep. Tomorrow's a big day."

"We could die tomorrow," she made a face.

"Uh…it's possible."

"And we haven't fucked yet."

Jeff's eyebrows rose. "No…no, we haven't."

"Not gonna die without fucking first."

"Huh." Jeff wasn't sure what to say. Or do.

Emma drew her tunic off. "Help me with this," she said, pointing to her bra.

"Uh...Emma, why don't we, you know, cuddle first?"

Emma pulled up short, as if she hadn't thought of that. "That...that's good. Cuddling is good."

Jeff lay down next to her and spooned with her, drawing her close to him, and savoring the smell of her hair.

"I like you," Emma said.

"I like you too."

"I don't know why I like you. You're not smart."

"Gee...thanks."

"Wait...I didn't mean it that way." She laughed at herself. "Don't take that...I goofed."

Jeff waited.

"What I mean is...I expected I would marry another scientist."

"I *am* a scientist. I have a doctorate in astrophysics. Plus a master's degree in military tactics. Although that's not, strictly speaking, scientific. Still...I'm no slouch in the education department."

"An astrophysicist. I didn't know." She sounded delighted. "Well, poop. You're not nearly as dangerous now."

"It's hard to know how to please you," Jeff confessed.

"I didn't want to die without...telling you how I feel." Emma said.

"And fucking," he added.

"It's all kind of...mixed up together."

"Uh-huh. So...tell me how you feel."

She hesitated. He wondered if it was as difficult for her to speak about her emotions as it was for him. She was a scientist, after all, more comfortable in the world of numbers and empirical facts than in the amorphous, ambiguous world of feelings.

"Emma?" he prompted.

Her breathing had become deep and slow. She started to snore.

It FELT good to sit in the captain's chair again. Jeff reveled in the strength and resilience of his "young" body. His mind buzzed with both excitement and information. The bridge was tiny, with just enough room to navigate between the various stations. Whereas larger bridges felt broad and expansive, this one felt stretched and narrow. He'd never commanded a research vessel like the *Kepler* before. His mind briefly flitted on the fact that, just a couple of weeks ago, Jo had been sitting in a chair identical to this one. He shook the thought from his mind and focused on the task before him. Emma covered the science station, looking bleary. She wouldn't admit to being hung-over, but it was hard to imagine she could be feeling otherwise.

"Take us out, Mr. Pho," Jeff said. "Declination minus thirty-eight point six, right ascension twelve hours, nineteen minutes, four seconds."

"Speed?" Martin Pho called over his shoulder. His black hair was cropped short, almost shaved, and his neck was weirdly thin. The kid was…angular.

"Maximum standard propulsion." The ship didn't have a superlux drive, so that was the best they could do. Jeff figured if they got a day out from Sol Station, away from any inhabited human outpost, that would be distance enough. Besides, it would give Emma and her team a chance to finish running their numbers. She'd asked for more time and been denied. The Prox weren't slowing down and every day they delayed…

Jeff shuddered. Just the trip out was a waste, in his opinion, however much of a godsend the extra time might seem to Emma. He didn't need the safety zone between them and other humans. He was confident. Since the accident, every test had gone perfectly. *I know what I'm doing, goddammit.*

But what if he didn't? A niggling voice pricked at the fringes of his soul, of his conscience, of his awareness. He beat it back with logic and a confidence cultivated from a lifetime of military training.

Jeff watched the star field whirl as their vessel banked to head out into uninhabited space. He liked earth. Hell, he even liked Sol Station. But he was never quite so much at home as when he was in a captain's chair.

"Reports," he called, looking up to check his neural for the lists of incoming data from the different stations. There were already three reports waiting for him. Others filed in. He did a cursory check and found everything in order. He silently dictated a message to the ship's medic. Then he rolled his eyes back down and rose, walking over to Emma's station. "The medic wants to see you," he said quietly.

"What?" Emma said, looking confused.

"That's an order," he said, with an amused lilt to his voice. He turned his back and walked back to his chair. She scowled at him but rose and left the bridge. She might be too proud to get some hangover relief, but he wasn't going to let it pass. A steroid, stimulant, and painkiller cocktail was exactly what she needed. He wanted to make sure his chief science officer was at her best.

He'd brought only one shift out, instead of the standard three. It would mean everyone would be on until they got back, but it was a short flight. For all his confidence, Jeff still wanted to minimize the risk for anyone aboard. Jennings had not objected, no doubt thinking the same.

Every day the reports from the colonies were tragic. The casualties were astronomical. Every military planner in the CDF was studying the transmissions and Jo's discoveries. A consensus was emerging on the earth's defensive strategy. Only one piece of the puzzle was missing, and everything was hanging on whether "Bowers' alien technology" (as it was widely referred to) was going to work. Jeff felt the pressure. And despite the risks and the calamity that had already befallen them, Jeff felt a confidence that he could not readily explain or defend.

Emma returned, shooting daggers at him with her eyes. He smiled at her and shot her a message.

—Feeling better?

—Asshole.

—That's "Captain Asshole" to you.

She ignored him and returned to her station.

The rest of the flight was uneventful, as Jeff suspected it would be. The *Kepler* was a sturdy, sound vessel, and the crew was young but capable. When alerted that they were closing in on the arbitrary periphery of the "safe zone" he had proposed, he left the rest of his meal sitting where it was in the mess and returned to the bridge. He nodded at his number one, a swarthy young woman named Camil Nira who was worthy of her own command. If they were successful, her promotion to captain seemed inevitable. He swung into his chair and called for reports. Looking up, he scanned them and found nothing amiss.

"Instructions, Captain?" Pho asked.

Jeff felt the eyes of the bridge crew on him. He met Emma's eyes and saw her smile at him. All was forgiven.

"Battle ready status."

Pho narrowed his eyes. "Battle ready, sir? This is a research vessel."

Jeff laughed. "I'm just...I'm imagining the kind of scenario that would play out if we're successful here. Our ships will need to be ready to leap into the fray the moment we...I...move them. So, let's keep everything up and running. This ship does have weapons—"

"Not enough to warrant a weaponer," Pho noted.

"Fine, but we've got two laser cannons, fore and aft. Or as I like to call them, cigarette lighters."

Pho chuckled and turned back to his station. "Weapons armed and ready, sir."

"Good. Mr. Wall, report on our status to Sol Station. Include a full datapacket with all reports from the last hour."

"Yes sir," the communications officer responded, her voice professional but unsteady. *She's scared,* Jeff thought. *Well, that's not unreasonable.*

"Dr. Stewart, do we have full sensors?"

"All sensors online and responsive," she affirmed. "Sir."

She was clearly not used to serving in a military capacity. He'd have to tease her about that later. *If there* is *a later*, he reminded himself.

"All right then. Let's go someplace...far."

He watched Pho stiffen just before he closed his eyes. He allowed himself to sink into that deep place where he was able to make contact with the All. Then he reached out with his mind toward the nearest neighboring star.

"Captain, an unknown vessel has just materialized off our port bow, range...60,000 kilometers."

Jeff's eyes snapped open. "On screen," he said.

The star field was quickly replaced by an image from a portside sensor. A looming, spherical vessel filled half the screen. "Mr. Wall, get us a better image on that."

The young communications officer adjusted the sensor, bringing the ship into sharper focus, and centering it in the middle of the viewscreen. Jeff rose and took a step and a half toward the viewscreen, all that the cramped bridge would allow. Jeff hadn't ever seen anything like it. It was not perfectly round—it was taller than it was wide, but not by much. At its center there appeared to be a bubble, or at least a smaller sphere set into the vessel that looked like it might be detachable. Radiating out of the bubble were wide flanges that created its circular appearance. It reminded Jeff of the ridges around the eyes of a baboon.

"Mr. Wall, review all ship designs in our database and get me a match. I need to know who this is."

"Aye, sir."

"Dr. Stewart, can you get me some measurements on that thing?"

Emma bit her lip as her fingers flew over her console. "It's...457.2 kilometers across...and deep. 475.8 kilometers high."

"That's a huge fucking ship," Jeff said. "That's almost a space station."

"A space station that moves very fast, I'm willing to bet," Pho added. "I'm getting an energy signal that I don't know how to interpret. It's off the...well, it's beyond the capacity of our sensors to measure."

"Their shields are up," Emma said. "And they're powering weapons."

"What weapons have they got?" Jeff asked. Not that it mattered. Whatever a ship like that might have, it was far superior to their own firepower. What they had was little more than a glorified can opener.

"Nothing that matches anything in our records," Emma said. "This is an alien vessel."

"Sir, I'm getting a communication on all channels."

"Put it through," Jeff said.

"It's audio only," Wall warned him.

A moment later a booming voice filled the bridge. "You. Must. Stop."

"Who are you?" Jeff asked.

"We. Are. The Ulim." The voice sounded like nothing Jeff had heard before. Then again, he'd never encountered an Ulim ship. Hell, "Danny" had said they didn't use them. Why would a species that can travel anywhere in the universe through the vacuum of space need a ship? And yet, here it was. Almost unbelievably large, possessing weapons and capabilities they could only guess at.

"Mr. Wall, make sure Sol Station is getting this via ansible. All of it."

"Sending them a catch-up datapacket now...and they're in real time." Wall said.

"You don't need a ship to talk to me," Jeff said to the viewscreen.

"It seems we need one for you to listen to us." The voice was softer. Not Danny's but...similar. It sounded human. There were notes of anger, concern, disappointment. *Or,* Jeff thought, *I'm just imagining all of that.* But he wasn't. The Ulim might be as different from humans as a species could be, physically, but their emotional life was rich and morally introspective. Jeff felt a kinship with them—the kinship of sentient species who feel and care.

"I have listened to you. The risk is necessary."

"You have already tasted the risk. It was bitter, we think."

Jeff couldn't deny that. And they were hitting below the belt. "We learn from our mistakes," he said.

"There is no returning from some mistakes," the voice said.

"We are determined to try again," Jeff informed them, defiantly.

"And we are determined to stop you."

"Captain, they are targeting weapons," Emma said.

Oh crap, Jeff thought, but he didn't say it out loud. *Keep them talking.* He knew them. What did he know that would make them hesitate, stop? "Is this what the Ulim desire? To be aggressors?"

"We are not aggressors. Circumstances require us to act. Sentient beings who cause harm to other beings must be stopped."

"We're not trying to hurt anyone. We're just trying to stay alive."

"You will hurt many."

"You don't know that."

"Yes. We do."

"You won't fire on us," Jeff said.

"Yes. We will."

"Weapons locked," Emma said.

Well, shit, Jeff thought. He stroked his chin, mind racing. He remembered his first meeting with them, something their Danny had said. "Coercion is not our way," he said out loud.

Jeff chewed on his lip. He looked around at his bridge crew. He knew what he had to do, but he had been wrong before. The risk was too great. *Or is it...?* Jeff's mind kept returning to that phrase, *Coercion is not our way.*

Like a mantra it shut everything else out of his mind—leaving no room for the self-hatred, the self-recriminations, the doubts and agonizing that had until now tyrannized him. The voices stopped. The self-chatter, the obsessive rumination, the guilt. All of it. Stopped. Hanging in mid-space, just like the Ulim ship, was one solitary thought, one sentence that pinned him like a butterfly to a spreading board.

Coercion is not our way.

"Sir?" Pho asked.

"Mr. Pho," Jeff straightened his uniform and sat on the edge of his captain's chair. "Ahead full speed. Aim for that little bubble in the center of their ship."

"Sir?" Pho's eyes widened.

"You heard me," Jeff said. "Set a collision course and give it everything she's got. Ram them, Mr. Pho."

CHAPTER TEN

Mr. Pho gulped.

"Mr. Pho, you have two choices." Jeff's voice was calm but menacing. "You can obey my order or you can face a court-martial when we get planetside."

Pho's eyes shifted to Mr. Wall, but she kept her eyes glued to her panel. Pho glanced next at Emma, desperate.

"Now, Mr. Pho, or I'll take the wheel myself."

Pho looked at Jeff again, straightened up, and turned back to his panel. "Ramming speed, sir."

Inside, Jeff let out a sigh of relief. Outside, however, he was as impassive as granite. "Take us straight through the pupil of whatever that glass bubble is smack dab in the middle of that ship."

"Course locked, sir. 200,000k…150,000k… 100,000k…50,000k…"

The Ulim ship filled the viewscreen now.

"Jeff, this is suicide!" Emma barked.

That's 'Captain,' here, Jeff thought, but he kept his focus squarely on the viewscreen.

"Counting down to impact," Pho said. "Impact in 5...4...3..."

Jeff clutched the arm of his captain's chair and pressed himself as far back in the chair as he could, feeling its solidity, seizing the illusion of safety its sturdiness afforded him.

"2...1...Impact."

But there was no impact. They'd headed straight for the bubble, gone into it...and through it.

Jeff hung his head, resting his chin on his chest, slouching down in his chair.

"We...we're not dead," Pho breathed incredulously.

"No, Mr. Pho. We're not dead. Mr. Wall, aft sensors. Show me the Ulim ship."

The picture on the viewscreen changed, but the scene didn't. Now they were staring at the backside of the Ulim vessel, looking exactly like a mirror image of her front. There were no thrusters, nothing you would expect to see on the underbelly of a ship. Just another front. It was an image, an illusion.

"How did you know, sir?" Pho asked.

"I didn't know, Mr. Pho. I strongly suspected, based on a conversation I had with the Ulim a couple mon—a long time ago."

"Remind me not to question your hunches."

Jeff smiled at that and swiveled in his seat, facing Emma. "Anyone need to go to the little girl's head?"

THE ULIM SHIP—OR at least, the illusion of it—had not moved, but that didn't matter. "Let's stop wasting time," Jeff announced to his bridge crew. "We've got a test to perform.

We've got a mission. We've got a lot of people counting on us. So let's get it done."

His bridge crew blinked. "Today, please," he added. Everyone sprung into action.

"Dr. Stewart, with me," he said.

Her eyebrows raised and she followed him off the bridge. Standing in the hallway, she waited until a crewmember scurried by. Then she gave him a half smile. "I thought you didn't need the chair."

"I don't. I just wanted to…" he kissed her.

At first she hesitated. Then she consented. More than consented, she reciprocated, meeting his tongue with hers, searching out the depths of his mouth, his passion, his soul. When he finally drew away, she was panting, eager for him again. "I care about you," he said.

"You can't bring yourself to say it, can you?"

"No….not yet."

She looked into his eyes, and gave him a sad smile. "Neither can I."

"What does this mean?" he asked.

"I think it means that now I can fuck you sober."

"Too bad we have to work," he smiled.

"It is. Too bad," she agreed. "Rain check?"

"Better than that," he said. "It's a date."

Before he could say anything else, she drew him down by his epaulets and kissed him again.

———

EMMA FITTED the new jack into his neural. "Okay?" she asked.

Jeff moved his head back and forth, feeling for any slack in the connection. There was none. "Okay," he answered. She nodded and returned to her station. Jeff settled back into the captain's chair, finding just the right position for maximum comfort. "Mr. Pho, you will have the con so long as I'm...incapacitated."

"Aye, sir," Pho said.

Jeff glanced over at Emma. She touched a couple of places on her console, then looked up at him and smiled. Then she blushed. Then she nodded. "All good here," she said. Then she added, "Captain. Sir."

His lip turned up slightly and he closed his eyes. "Let's get this done."

Pho sat straight upright in his seat. "We got trouble."

"What now?" Jeff snapped, then internally cursed himself for it.

"Another ship materializing off the portside bow. Er... same ship...I think."

Jeff jerked up, then felt the pain in the back of his neck when the patch to his neural went taught. "Ouch," he said. Emma scrambled to the captain's chair, but he waved her off and began barking orders. "I want a gravitic reading this time," he said.

Emma rushed back to her post. "Can't be in two places at once," she complained. Jeff smiled at that, involuntarily. Inside he was kicking himself for not getting a gravitational reading on the last ship. But then he expected a ship to be a ship—at first, at least.

Emma's fingers flew over her panel. "It has mass," she said. "47 million tons plus change, which is about what you'd expect from a ship that large."

"That's what I wanted to know." He didn't expect them to try the same trick twice. The first one was a feint. This one was for real. Still, deep in his gut, he didn't expect the Ulim to fire on them.

"They're powering weapons, sir," Pho said.

Then again, he could be wrong. Jeff scowled. He'd played chess with people smarter than him...and won. He tried to force himself to think creatively, but it was no good. He felt beaten.

Then he felt his body shift. The air around him became luminous. His surroundings faded and were replaced by an infinite nothingness of white. He was *inside*. He and the Ulim were one.

He caught motion out of the corner of his eye and turned his head. He was surprised to discover that he had a head. Danny was there. He did not look pleased.

"That was a foolhardy move," he said. He looked exactly the way he did before they had shipped out to Catskill, exactly as Jeff liked to remember him.

"Perhaps it was. But I was right."

"What if you hadn't been?"

Jeff shrugged. "At least I wouldn't be around to beat myself up about it."

"You have not healed."

Jeff blinked. "My scars are my armor," he managed.

"Your scars are your undoing."

"Is that a threat?"

"The Ulim do not threaten. The Ulim do not lie. The Ulim do not coerce."

"What do you call this, then? I call kidnapping coercion, don't you?"

"We have not kidnapped you. Your body is still aboard. We just wanted to...to talk."

"In that case, I'm done talking."

"You must see reason."

"I must give in and let the crab bastards eat us? I don't think so."

"You must find another way."

"Then give me another way."

They stared at one another. Danny pulled at his chin in a very human gesture of frustration.

"I'm not hearing a wealth of options," Jeff prompted. When Danny said nothing, Jeff said. "Look, it's been swell catching up. It's time for me to get back to my ship."

He closed his eyes and willed the calm to descend over his mind. He felt the presence of the Ulim, his unity with them, their omniscience and omnipresence. He reached beyond the coziness of their shared mind and found his ship, dwarfed by another. He saw his own body, jacked in, looking peaceful, asleep, maybe dead. He paused to truly "see" Emma. He saw her emotional desperation, her affection for him, her fear. Everything he suspected was true. He widened his focus to take in his crew, saw their confusion, their fear for what might happen next, their pride in serving, their deep desire to save their people. He shared it, all of it.

He drew on the power jacked into his neural. It was a blue-white energy that made everything in him buzz. It was clean—too clean. It was addictive. He widened his awareness in every direction, soon encountering Earth. He took in the lives and fears and feelings of twelve billion souls, suffering with them, triumphing with them, feeling with them. It did not exhaust him.

"Do not do this," Danny said. It was only his voice this time, as Jeff had moved well beyond form. He ignored him and drew on the power again—drew it deeply, sucking at it as if it were a fire hose and he was the thirstiest god on Olympus. When the blue fire turned acid white, obscuring everything but its own terrible power, he reached out toward the wild, compact energy of Alpha Centauri.

He not only saw it, he embraced it, enveloped it, *felt* it.

He opened the metaphorical fingers of one hand and grasped it—at precisely the optimal orbit for their position. Then he looked backward and gripped the space surrounding *The Kepler*. Then in his mind, he ignored the space between, negated it, *oned* it with the space held in both of his hands.

The energy cracked with a boom that nearly made him lose his grip, but he held on. Then he released it, feeling the elasticity of space exert itself once again. He felt a moment of vertigo, a disorientation that resolved itself in seconds, leaving him in his chair, surrounded by his crew, orbiting a yellow-orange star.

EPILOGUE

When Jeff opened his eyes, his crew seemed frozen. Their mouths hung open, their eyes were wide as eggs. Jeff reached back and jerked the neural connector out of his port. He stood. Then the crew erupted into applause. "Not now, goddam it," he barked. "Reports."

They each turned back to their stations and he saw their fingers flying. A couple of them looked up, checking stats on their neurals, and then moments later sending reports. The red light in his own peripheral vision indicated they were coming in.

He steadied himself on his command chair as he scanned them. A T-joint needed to be replaced on deck three. It had been registering as needing to be replaced since they began. All was normal. "Mr. Wall, send a datapacket back to Sol Station, give 'em everything we've got. Drown them in data. We don't want anyone saying they don't have the whole story."

"Reports are still coming in, sir. It'll take me about fifteen minutes to send it off."

Jeff waved in her direction. "Just so long as it goes. In the meantime, I think it's time for champagne, don't you?"

He saw a smile break out on Wall's face as she turned back to her panel. He turned to his right and caught Emma's eye. She nodded at him, clearly pleased and proud. It wasn't just pride in him, he knew. There was more to what was shining on her face than that. It was hope. They had a chance against those crab bastards after all.

"Um…sir?"

"Yes, Mr. Pho."

"I just ran a stellar cartographical check to make sure we're…where we think we are."

"I know exactly where we are, Lieutenant."

"Uh…I'm not questioning that, sir. It's just—"

"Just what, Mr. Pho?"

"I think we should hold off on the champagne for a bit. I've found some anomalies."

"What kind of anomalies?" He looked over at Emma, saw the crease in her brow as she began to run some tests of her own. He resented Mr. Pho interrupting his moment of triumph, but hell, it was his job to be thorough.

"Ninety-eight percent of the star field matches our records. Everything is exactly where the star charts say they should be."

"You mean *almost* everything is exactly where it should be?" Jeff clarified.

"Er…yes sir, that's what I mean. The other 2 percent… doesn't match what's on the charts."

"What are you saying, Mr. Pho?"

"One percent of the stars are missing, and one percent are…well, there're stars where there shouldn't be."

A note from the authors:

THANKS *so much for reading our book—we hope you enjoyed it, and that you will continue the story in* Oblivion Flight.

And if you can, please post an honest review at amazon or whichever site you purchase books from. It doesn't have to be long, just a sentence or two with your feelings and opinions. It helps authors so much when you leave a review, and we'd be so grateful for yours! Thank you for taking the time, and thanks for reading!

—J.R. Mabry & B.J. West

Continue the adventure in the next
thrilling novel in the Oblivion saga:

OBLIVION FLIGHT
by J.R. Mabry & B.J. West

A scientific experiment goes horribly wrong.
The earth…the galaxy…the universe is destroyed.
And there's only one person to blame…you.

Get *Oblivion Flight* today!

Made in the USA
Monee, IL
19 February 2021